Rachael Thomas has always loved reading romance, and is thrilled to be a Mills & Boon author. She lives and works on a farm in Wales—a far cry from the glamour of a Mills & Boon Modern Romance story—but that makes slipping into her characters' worlds all the more appealing. When she's not writing, or working on the farm, she enjoys photography and visiting historical castles and grand houses. Visit her at rachaelthomas.co.uk.

Books by Rachael Thomas

Mills & Boon Modern Romance

The Sheikh's Last Mistress
New Year at the Boss's Bidding
From One Night to Wife
Craving Her Enemy's Touch
Claimed by the Sheikh
A Deal Before the Altar

Brides for Billionaires

Married for the Italian's Heir

The Billionaire's Legacy

To Blackmail a Di Sione

Visit the Author Profile page at
millsandboon.co.uk for more titles.

A CHILD
CLAIMED BY GOLD

BY
RACHAEL THOMAS

First Published in Great Britain 2016
By Mills & Boon, an imprint of HarperCollins*Publishers*
1 London Bridge Street, London, SE1 9GF

© 2016 Rachael Thomas

ISBN: 978-0-263-92389-6

Printed and bound in Spain
by CPI, Barcelona

'I wouldn't lie to you, Nikolai,' Esmia said defensively, and looked away from his dark eyes and feigned interest in the tall buildings clearly visible above the newly green trees of the park.

Maybe if she took a few shots from the carriage he'd see she was as unaffected by him as he appeared to be by her.

The lens of the camera clicked, but she had no idea what she'd taken. Concentration was impossible with his dominating presence opposite her and the looming discussion of their baby. She turned the camera off and looked at him, to see he'd been watching every move she'd made.

'We need to talk about our predicament.'

So his dark eyes watched her, assessing her reaction to his words.

'Predicament?' she snapped, giving him her full attention. 'Is that what this baby is to you? A *predicament*? Something else you have to deal with? Just what do you suggest, Nikolai?'

'It's a predicament.'

He said it calmly. Far too calmly. And it unnerved her. What was coming next?

'One I intend to solve, but to do so we must...'

One Night With Consequences

When one night…leads to pregnancy!

When succumbing to a night of unbridled desire
it's impossible to think past the morning after!

But, with the sheets barely settled, that little blue line
appears on the pregnancy test and it doesn't take long
to realise that one night of white-hot passion
has turned into a lifetime of consequences!

Only one question remains:

How do you tell a man you've just met
that you're about to share more than just his bed?

Find out in:

**Look for more One Night With Consequences
coming soon!**

CHAPTER ONE

Nikolai Cunningham braced himself against the icy-cold winds of the homeland he'd turned his back on as he waited for Emma Sanders to arrive on the next train. The heavy grey sky held the promise of more snow and matched his anger that a complete stranger had interfered in his life, bringing him back to Russia and a family he'd long ago disowned. He and his mother had left Vladimir for New York when he was ten years old and the shadow of the events preceding that day still clung to them, threatening to unravel everything.

The train rumbled into the station and he prepared himself for what he was certain would be the worst few days imaginable. His life was in New York, and returning to Vladimir had never been part of his plans. That was until his estranged grandmother had crept from the past, offering her family story to *World in Photographs*.

He'd also been contacted, no doubt because his grandmother had very graciously provided the name he now lived under, but he'd refused. At least, until he'd learnt his grandmother was more than ready to talk and expose everything he and his mother had fled from, probably putting the blame firmly at his mother's feet. In a bid to protect his mother from their painful past, and prevent his name being linked to the family name of Petrushov once more, he'd had no option but to return.

He stood back and watched the travellers climbing down from the train, scanning them quickly, trying to remember the image he'd seen of Miss Sanders on the Internet and match it to one of the disembarking passengers. Then he saw her, wrapped up against the cold in true Russian style, only her face visible between the *faux* fur hat and scarf. She looked about her nervously, clutching the handle of her small case in a gloved hand. She could have been Russian, she blended in so well, but her apprehension and uncertainty singled her out as a stranger to Vladimir.

Accepting he had to do this and face whatever came from it for his mother's sake, he pulled his coat collar tighter against the cold and walked towards her. She looked at him and he held her gaze as he strode along the platform, the determination to get this over with as fast as possible dominating all other thought.

'Miss Sanders.' He stopped in front of her, registering her height, which almost matched his, something he found strangely pleasing.

'Mr Petrushov?' Her voice was as clear and crisp as a frosty morning, but by contrast her eyes were a mossy green, reminding him of the depths of Russian forests in summer. Why was he noticing such details? She distracted him, knocked him off course, and only now he registered how she'd addressed him.

Nikolai's anger intensified. Beautiful or not, Miss Sanders obviously hadn't done her research well. It had been seventeen years since he'd abandoned the name Petrushov in favour of his stepfather's name, Cunningham.

'Nikolai Cunningham,' he corrected then, before any questions could be asked, continued, 'I trust you enjoyed your train journey from Moscow?'

'Sorry—and yes, I did, Mr Cunningham.' He saw her dark brows furrow in confusion, but refused to elaborate on why he, a Russian-born man, had a distinctly American surname. That was none of her business and he had every intention it would stay that way.

He looked down at the young woman, wrapped up against the cruel winds of winter, and although her alluring green eyes were a distraction he was unable to put aside his anger towards her. 'And you must be Miss Sanders from *World in Photographs*?' He added silently to himself, *the woman who wants to rip open my mother's past and delve into my childhood, no doubt in order to further her career.*

'Please, call me Emma,' she said and held out her gloved hand to him. He didn't take it but looked into the lustrous green of her eyes and wondered what colour her hair was beneath the fur of her hat. Her photo on the Internet hadn't done her any justice: she was stunning.

Irritation mingled with the anger. This was the last woman he wanted to stir his interests. Just being here in Vladimir meant she had the power to cause real hurt to his mother and he strongly suspected she didn't know yet just how much. It was up to him to ensure she never realised just how dramatic the true story of his family was.

He fully intended that she would be distracted by the undeniable beauty of a Russian winter and had already organised plenty of photo opportunities to keep her from the real story. A story that would destroy his mother and upend his world if it got out. All he had to do was prevent her meeting with the grandmother he hadn't seen since he was ten but he didn't yet know how to achieve that.

'We should get out of the wind,' he said firmly, trying to ignore the way the colour of her eyes reminded him of his childhood summers here in Vladimir. It was a place he hadn't thought of for a long time and certainly didn't want to think of now. 'I took the liberty of booking into the same hotel; that way, I can be of as much help to you as possible.'

His motives were much less honourable. All he intended to do was ensure she saw only what he wanted her to see and certainly not what he feared his grandmother wanted to share with her—a family torn apart by deceit.

'Thank you.' She smiled up at him and satisfaction made him return the smile. He was already winning her round. Just a few more days of this nonsense and he could head back to New York and put all this behind him. 'That's very thoughtful of you.'

'The hotel has a very comfortable lounge where I suggest we go over just what you need for your article.'

She believed he was being thoughtful. What would she say if she knew he was determined to hide all he could, despite his grandmother's attempt to ruin the family name? That was another matter he had to deal with and one thing was for certain: Miss Emma Sanders wouldn't be a witness to that particular showdown.

'That would be a good idea.' She laughed softly and, although the scarf around her face hid her lips and she drew her shoulders up against the cold, from the way her eyes sparkled he could imagine she was smiling at him. The image stirred sensations which contrasted wildly with the anger and irritation he'd been harbouring since discovering that his grandmother had agreed to be interviewed for the magazine.

'Allow me,' he said and reached for her luggage, pleased it was a small case and her photography bag. This meant she didn't have any intentions to make her stay any longer than the three days *World in Photographs* had requested from him and his family.

His family. That was a joke.

'Thank you.' This time, as she pulled her scarf a little lower with gloved hands, he could see she was smiling. It also had an unexpected effect on him. The idea of kissing those lips flashed through his mind, sending a trail of blazing lust hurtling through him. That train of thought would achieve nothing and he grimly pushed it away. This was not a time to allow lust to reign and certainly not with this woman.

'This way, Miss Sanders,' he said purposefully, ignoring her invitation to use her first name, and walked briskly away without ensuring she was following, heading for the hotel he'd booked into. He'd purposefully chosen the same hotel as the interfering Miss Sanders, enabling him to ensure she didn't meddle in the dark, hidden past of his family. Had that been the right decision?

Now that he'd met Emma Sanders he knew he'd be able to charm and distract her, making sure she learnt only the romantic ideals about his family story she was no doubt searching for. The only problem was that he suspected he himself was in danger of falling victim to her charms and distractions.

'I expect you are used to this cold, but it's a shock for me,' she said as they stepped inside, out of the wind. The warmth of the hotel, set out as if a village of cosy log cabins, gave it an intimate and even romantic feel that would no doubt help his cause. Very soon he'd have Miss Emma Sanders believing he was more than pleased to talk about his family history.

'My home is in New York, Miss Sanders.'

'Oh,' she said, pulling off her hat as they entered the lounge area of the main part of the hotel, the heat of the log fire a welcome relief from outside. 'I'm sorry; I assumed you lived here with your grandmother.'

He watched as she removed her scarf, revealing long, straight hair the colour of sable, and for a brief moment he forgot himself, forgot that this woman had the power to hurt his mother and expose him for what he really was, as that earlier trail of lust streaked through him again. Mentally he shook himself. He might have a history of brief and hot affairs with women, but this was one woman he could not want.

'Never assume anything, Miss Sanders.' Angered by his reaction at seeing beneath the layers of dark fur she wore, as if born to Russian winters, he fought to keep his tone neutral. She was a beautiful woman, and his body's reaction to her meant that his voice was anything but neutral and much harsher than it should have been.

She looked up at him, a question in her eyes, her slender dark brows furrowed into a frown of confusion. 'Life has taught me that, Mr Petrushov.'

'Cunningham,' he corrected her again, but something in the way she said those words and the look of haunted fear which had rushed across her beautiful face as she'd spoken nudged at his conscience. He shouldn't be so hard, so aggressive. Not if he wanted to steer her away from the truth of his family. Maybe playing to the attraction sizzling between them would be the way to create that distraction?

He wondered what she meant as he picked up on the inference that life hadn't been easy for her. He resisted the urge to ask, not wanting to draw her into a conversation that may turn back on him. Over the years he'd become adept at providing just enough information about himself to satisfy people, but never enough for them to know the full facts.

'Then we already understand one another.' He pulled off his coat and hat, hung them up then took hers from her, his fingers unexpectedly brushing against hers. A jolt of heat surged through him and, as she pulled her hand back, she looked up at him, her green eyes wide and startled. Her full lips, slicked with gloss, parted and he had an almost uncontrollable urge to lower his head and kiss her. Not a gentle brushing of lips but a hard, demanding kiss. The kind of kiss which led to fierce and passionate sex.

What the hell was he thinking?

She stepped back away from him as a flush of colour covered her pale face and her eyes darkened to resemble the deepest ocean. She'd felt it too, of that there was no doubt. If she had been any other woman, he wouldn't have thought twice about acting on the attraction. But she wasn't any other woman. She could tear open his past, threatening not just his mother's happiness but his reputation. He wouldn't allow it to happen—not at any cost.

'Yes, yes, we do. We—we understand each other

perfectly.' She stumbled over her words and he stifled a smile of satisfaction. Maybe the attraction could be used to ensure she didn't find out just who he really was. If a touch and a brief moment of sexual chemistry could disarm her, that would be a pleasant way to distract her from digging around too much into his family's past.

Emma hated the way she could hardly form a sentence as Nikolai Cunningham all but scrutinised her. He had muddled her mind and sent her insides into turmoil from the moment they'd met. It was as if a spark of recognition had reached out from him, inexplicably drawing her closer.

She thought of Richard, the man she'd always wished could be more than just a friend, and compared him to this powerful specimen of masculinity. Richard was attractive but safe, but this man was undeniably handsome and oozed a lethal kind of sex appeal. She shivered as something arced between them. He held her gaze and she knew she had to remember he was also the man who held the key to her successfully completing this assignment and securing a long-term contract with *World in Photographs*.

What happened over the next few days could launch her career as a photographer. More importantly, it would provide a regular income, which was badly needed if she was to stand any chance at all of supporting her younger sister Jess as she embarked on a lifetime dream of becoming a ballerina. They'd both had so many knockbacks in life, going from foster home to foster home, that she wanted her younger sister to do what made her happy. And she was good at it—talented, in fact. After the things they'd experienced together, they both deserved happiness, and if Jess was happy then so was she.

The tall, dark-haired man who'd just sent a frisson of awareness zipping around her had been distinctly cold towards her initially, more so than the icy winds. Something had inexplicably changed in the last few moments. He'd looked at her differently, making heat surge through her in a way she'd never known before, and she wasn't sure she was able to deal with it. Thoughts of Richard had never done that to her.

'I shall accompany you to the meeting with Marya Petrushov, who is my grandmother, but first I will take you to several locations you can use for the photographs you require.' Something about the tone of his voice made it clear that to ask for more than this right now would be inadvisable, especially the way he'd said his grandmother's name. She immediately sensed unresolved issues and wondered how often he saw his grandmother with so many miles between them.

Throwing caution to the wind and quelling her curiosity for now, she looked directly at him, her chin lifted slightly, and clearly set out her terms. 'I not only need photographs of locations, Mr Petrushov, but of you and your grandmother—along with any other family members.'

Her brief was to step inside the life of the Russian family which had made its wealth only decades ago and see just how it lived. If she didn't deliver on that brief, she'd never get her contract, which would mean she'd have no way of funding Jess in one of Russia's elite ballet schools. The fact that this meeting was taking place in a town only a night-train-ride away from

where Jess had a much-coveted place at a world fa-
mous ballet school was a good sign and she'd believed
it couldn't go wrong, that it was meant to be.

Now, looking at Nikolai as he laid down his own
rules about the interview, she had serious doubts it
would ever go right. He dominated the entire room
they'd walked into; even though the residents' lounge
was large and spacious, he had taken command of
every bit of that space. He was undoubtedly in control.

He also intimidated her, not that she would ever let
him know that. It wouldn't do to let a man who was
obviously used to being in charge see subservience.
No, she would stand her ground. She sensed she would
have to be as strong as him if she wanted to get what
the brief dictated.

'There are no other family members, Miss Sanders.' He made his way towards a group of comfortable
chairs around the warmth of the fire and she followed,
determined he wasn't going to put her off so easily. She
only had a week here in Russia and she wanted to see
Jess before flying back to London.

He gestured to her to sit and then took the chair
next to hers, his long legs suddenly emphasised as he
sat. Nerves filled her and the way he watched her unsettled her more than she'd ever known. She wished
she knew what he was thinking, but those dark eyes
of his were unreadable.

'A photo of you and your grandmother…' She hadn't
even finished her suggestion when he leant forward,
bringing them close to one another in an intimate kind
of way. It was too close and her words faltered into
nothing.

'No.' That one word silenced any suggestions she

had, the anger in it reverberating around the room like a rogue firework. Then, as if he realised how hard and unyielding that sounded, he sat back and offered an explanation. 'I have not seen my grandmother for many years, so a loving family photo will not be possible, Miss Sanders.'

This wasn't going well. With each passing second, her dream of easily pulling together the article and then slipping away to Perm to see Jess for a few days was rapidly disintegrating. The wild and untamed look in his eyes as he regarded her suspiciously left her in no doubt that he meant what he said.

'Look, Mr Petrushov—sorry, Cunningham.' Now, to make matters worse, she'd called him by his family name again and, judging by the tightness of his jaw, that was not something which would endear her to him. She pressed on, not sure this whole situation could get any worse. 'I don't know what your problem is with me, but I am here to do a job. Your grandmother agreed with *World in Photographs* to be interviewed and photographed for the magazine and my job is to ensure that happens.'

She glared up at him, hoping to match his dominance with her determination, and wondered why she'd ever agreed to take on the interview role when photography was her field. The answer to that was her commitment to allowing her sister to follow her dreams.

He looked at her, his gaze slowly searching her face, lingering just a little too long on her lips. Tension crackled in the air around them and she was totally unaware of anything except the two of them. Mentally she shook herself free of it. Now was not a good time to become attracted to a man, and certainly not this man.

All through her teenage years she'd steadfastly held on to to a vow never to succumb to the temptation of a man. She'd managed that until she'd met Richard, a fellow photographer and the first man to pay her any kind of attention. She'd hoped their friendship would turn into something more, but two years down the line nothing had changed, and she watched in disillusion from the sidelines as he dated other women.

'And it is my duty to ensure my family isn't upset by your intrusion into our life, Miss Sanders.' He spoke slowly, his dark eyes hard and glittering, a very clear warning laced into every word. How could she be intruding when the old lady had agreed to be interviewed?

'I have no wish to upset anyone.' She looked up at him, into those midnight-black eyes, and knew she couldn't fight fire with fire. Her life with her mother, before she and Jess had been put into care, had taught her that. If she tried to match his strength and determination, she'd never get this assignment done. She lowered her gaze and looked down at her hands before looking back up from beneath her lashes. 'I apologise. Can we start again?'

The request completely stunned Nikolai. Moments ago she'd been brimming with fire. Passionate indignation had burned in her eyes, making his fight not to give in to the temptation to kiss her almost impossible. Now within seconds she'd become soft and compliant. Such a drastic changed filled him with suspicion. She was playing games with him.

'You want to go back into the cold and shake hands?'

He couldn't resist teasing her and was rewarded with a light flush of pink to her cheeks.

'No.' She laughed softly and her smile made her eyes shine, as if the sun was breaking through the forest and bouncing off fresh, green, spring leaves. 'I think we should start again with our conversation. Let's have a hot drink and discuss how we can both help each other out.'

Now he really was surprised. She was up to something, trying to manipulate the situation round to what she wanted. It was what the woman he should have married had always done and he'd been fool enough to let her—until he'd ended the charade that had been their engagement. She'd only wanted him for what he could provide for her.

'I don't think there is anything you can offer that will help me, Miss Sanders, but we will have a drink, and I will tell you how the next few days are going to work.'

Before she could say anything else, he signalled to a member of staff and ordered tea—something he wouldn't have requested in New York but, being back in Russia, his childhood memories were resurfacing in an unsettling way. Until he saw the flicker of interest in her eyes, he hadn't registered he'd used the first language he'd spoken as a child before his world had been torn apart by the pain of his mother's secret.

A secret that now haunted him. It was the same secret he suspected his grandmother wanted to unleash in the article and, just like her son, his cruel father, she was spiteful enough to manipulate him back to Russia to witness it all.

'Please, call me Emma,' she said, leaning back in

the chair opposite him, her jeans, tight around long, shapely legs, snagging his attention, filling his mind with thoughts he had no right to be thinking. 'And may I call you Nikolai?'

'Nikolai, yes,' he replied sharply. He had wanted to change his name to Nik when he'd left Russia as a young child—it had been his way of distancing himself from his father's family—but his mother had begged him to keep Nikolai, telling him she'd chosen the name because it was a family name and that he should keep some of his Russian roots.

'I get the distinct impression that you are not at all willing for me to talk to your grandmother, Nikolai— and yet it was her who approached *World in Photographs*, which makes me think there is something you don't want told.'

'How very shrewd.' And he'd thought he was going to turn on the charm and make her bend to his will. It seemed he'd greatly underestimated this woman. Her act of innocent shyness was exactly that. An act. Just like his ex, she was able to be whatever was necessary to get what she wanted.

'Perhaps we can come to some sort of agreement, one that will give me enough information to complete my job and afford your family enough privacy.' She sat back in her chair and looked at him, her dark brows raised in a silent show of triumph. If that was what she thought she'd achieved, he'd let her think that— for now.

'On one condition.' He picked up his tea, took a sip then met her gaze. He looked into her eyes and for the briefest of moments thought he'd seen anxiety. No, more than that—fear.

'And what is that condition?'

'That you tell me why this job is so important to you. Why come all the way from London to Vladimir for the ramblings of an old woman?' He had no idea if his grandmother rambled; he hadn't seen her for almost twenty-three years. It had been the day of his father's funeral and as a bemused ten-year-old he'd had no idea what was going on. No idea why his grandmother had turned him and his mother out. It was only six years later he'd learnt the disturbing truth and had vowed to do all he could to protect his mother from any further pain. A vow he fully intended to keep now.

'I took the job because it was a way of coming to Russia. It was as if fate was giving me the perfect opportunity. My sister, Jess, has a place at Perm Ballet School and once I've got what I need I'm going to spend a few days with her.' Her lovely green eyes filled with genuine excitement and that familiar pang of injustice almost stifled him. She'd had a happy childhood, had formed bonds with her sister, but his had been far from that thanks to one brutal act by his father, a man he had no wish to acknowledge as such.

'Your sister is here? In Russia?' This was the last thing he'd expected to discover and certainly hadn't turned up when he'd had Emma Sanders's background checked out. She had debts and she was far from well-known in the field of photography. Other than that, he'd found nothing of any significance. Nothing he could manipulate to make this situation work for him.

'Yes, ballet is her dream, and I intend to see that she can follow it.' Her face lit up and pride filled her voice and he saw an entirely different woman from the one he'd met outside just a short while ago. 'She's only sixteen and taking this job means I will be able to see her sooner than we'd planned, even if it's just a few days before I head back to London.'

At least now he could understand why she'd taken the job. Initially his suspicious mind had come to conclusions that weren't even there. She simply hadn't enough money to fly to Russia and see her sister so had taken the job. He did, however, still have doubts as to his grandmother's motives for instigating it all. Just what was she hoping to achieve? But, worse than that, how far was Emma prepared to go in order to impress *World in Photographs* in an attempt to launch her career?

'Then we can help one another, Emma. I can take you to places linked with my family's past where you can take as many photographs as you desire.' He paused, unsure why he'd used that word. Was it because of the way her body distracted him, making him want her? Colour heightened her cheeks again, making her appear shy and innocent, and he wondered if she understood the underlying sexual tension which was definitely building between them.

'And can I meet your grandmother? Ask her a few questions?' Her voice had become a little husky and she bit down on her lower lip, an action he wouldn't read into. Not if he wanted to stay in control of this nonsense and thwart his grandmother's attempt at stirring up trouble once more.

'Yes, but first we'll go to the places that are linked to my family. I have already made the arrangements for tomorrow.'

She looked happy, as if he'd just handed her a free pass. 'In that case, I will look forward to spending a few days with you.'

The irritating thing was, he also found himself looking forward to being with her. The very woman he'd wanted to despise on sight and he was undeniably attracted to her.

CHAPTER TWO

THE NEXT MORNING Emma was full of excitement and it wasn't just that, after a shaky start, this assignment, thanks to Nikolai's plans, would be done quickly and she could head off to meet Jess. She was taken aback to realise she was also excited to see Nikolai Cunningham again. After yesterday afternoon in his company, she was convinced he couldn't be as severe as he'd first appeared when she'd stepped off the train. Then he'd created such a formidable picture of power and command and she'd wished she'd been able to photograph him as he'd stood there, glaring at her.

It unnerved her to admit the excitement hadn't dissipated after they'd met and he'd shown her to his car. If anything it had increased and she had no idea why. After wasting several years worshipping Richard from afar and not being noticed, she didn't want to fall for the charms of another man—especially one as unattainable as Nikolai Cunningham.

'Where are we going now?' The large black car seemed to have glided silently through the white landscape and she'd wished many times she could stop and take photographs. Not for the magazine, but for herself. Her creative mind was working overtime and she saw images as if through the lens all over the place.

'To the place I knew as home until I was ten years old. It's just on the outskirts of Vladimir.' He looked straight ahead as he drove, his profile set into firm, determined lines. She had the distinct impression it was the last place he wanted to go and wondered at his motives for taking her there. He didn't strike her as a compliant man. Far from it.

'And who lives there now? Your grandmother?' she couldn't help but ask. The brief for the assignment and the need to be professional, to get the job done and leave on time, pushed to the forefront of her mind. She had to get this right, had to put the spin on it the magazine wanted, but everything she'd seen or been told so far was in total contrast to what she was supposed to portray. This wasn't a happy-ever-after story, unless you counted the global success of Nikolai's banking business that he'd created to complement his stepfather's exclusive real-estate business.

His silence deepened and she turned her attention to the road ahead. Moments later the car turned off onto a snow-covered lane that had no tracks on it at all, no hint that anyone had gone that way recently. Was the house empty?

Nikolai spoke harshly, in what she assumed was Russian, and most definitely sounded like a curse. She looked from him to the crumbling façade ahead of what must have once been a great house. It had rounded towers, some with turrets and others with pointed roofs, which reached into the grey sky above. The black holes, where once windows of assorted sizes had looked out over the flat landscape, seemed like watchful eyes.

Emma's heart went out to Nikolai as she pieced together the small amount she knew about him. None of it made sense, but it was obvious he hadn't expected this empty shell. She'd planned to take photographs of the place he'd grown up in, maybe even convince him to be in one, but now none of that felt right.

He got out of the car, seemingly unaware of her presence, and for a moment she sat and watched him. Then the photographer in her made that impossible for long. The image of his solitary figure, dressed in dark clothes, standing and looking at the neglected building, stark against the white landscape, was too much of a temptation. She had to take the photo.

Quietly, so as not to disturb him, she got out of the car, her camera in hand. The snow crunched under her boots as she moved a little closer. Seconds later she began taking photos. He remained oblivious to the clicks of the lens and as she looked back through the images she knew she wouldn't be using them for the article. These told a story of pain and loss and they were for her alone.

'This is where my family lived before my father died.' He didn't turn to speak to her, as if doing so would give away his emotions. Was he afraid of appearing weak? His tone had an icy edge to it, but she waited for him to continue. 'This is the first time I've seen it since I was a ten-year-old boy. My mother and I left for a new life in New York after that.'

'That must have been hard.' She moved instinctively towards him, but the cold glare in his eyes as he finally turned to face her warned against it. She just wanted him to know that she understood what it felt like to be displaced in life, not to know who you really were. Just like her and Jess, he'd been pushed from one adult to another and had known great sadness.

'Hard?' Nikolai could barely control his anger—not just at this woman, who was bringing all he'd thought he'd forgotten about his childhood back out for inspection, but also at his grandmother for instigating it. 'I don't think you could possibly know.'

He thought she'd say something, defend herself, but instead she shrugged, walked back to the car and took out her camera bag. He watched as she set up her tripod and again started to take photos of the old house. The camera clicked and, each time he heard it, it was as if it was opening yet another memory.

'Do you have any happy memories of this place?' She looked at him. Against the white snow and grey sky she looked stunning and he allowed this to distract him from the past. He didn't want to go there, not for anyone.

It was too late. A sense of terror crept over him as he saw himself, a young boy of eight, hiding beneath the antique table his father had been so proud to buy with his new-found wealth. He'd gone there seeing it as a place of safety, sure his father's temper wouldn't hurt his latest prized possession. He'd been wrong, very wrong. As his mother had begged and pleaded for his father to leave him alone, he'd been dragged out from beneath the table and lifted off his feet. He'd wriggled like mad, kicking and squealing, desperate to get away, yet knowing if he did his father would turn his attention to his mother. It was him or her and, in a bid to save her from at least one beating, he'd snarled words of hatred at his father. After that he couldn't remember what had happened.

He didn't want to.

He pushed the memories back. Analysing them wouldn't help anyone now, least of all himself.

'Not here, no,' he replied sternly and walked over to Emma, who was looking over her shoulder as she viewed the images she'd taken. The house didn't look so insidious on the screen of the camera, as if viewing it through the lens had defused the terrible memories of living there with his mother and father.

Emma's scent drifted up through the crisp air to meet him and he closed his eyes as summer flowers triggered happier memories. 'I was happiest in the summer, when we visited my mother's family.'

Why had he said that? Inwardly he berated himself for giving her information she could act on. At the thought of the country home his mother's parents had kept, he realised it was the perfect place to take her. He could hire a troika and sit back and watch as the romance of Russia unfolded. What woman wouldn't resist such a romantic story? It would be just what he needed to charm her away from the dark secrets he had to keep hidden away.

'Where was that? Close by?' Her interest was caught and she looked up at him, smiling and looking happier than he'd seen her since she'd arrived on the train. Then she looked vulnerable—beautiful and vulnerable.

'It is, yes.' He could hardly answer her as the attraction wound itself round him, drawing him ever closer to her.

'Can we go there?' she asked tentatively, her genuine smile and soft blush doing untold things to him. Why, he didn't know. He much preferred his women to be bold, dramatic and experienced at mutually beneficial affairs. Instinctively he knew Emma was not like that at all. She was the sort of woman who'd planned out a happy-ever-after, even as a small child. Definitely not for him.

'We will go tomorrow,' he said, stepping back from the temptation of this woman.

The next morning, as instructed by Nikolai, Emma waited, wearing her warmest clothes and even more excited than yesterday. Somehow they had drawn closer with each passing hour yesterday and, even though he didn't talk to her about the past and let her into his thoughts, he had shown her many wonderful places and she already had lots of images.

She also realised she liked him—perhaps a little too much. If she was honest, she was attracted to him in a way she hadn't known before, not even with Richard.

'Ready?' he said as he met her in the hotel reception.

Like a child about to be shown a Christmas tree, she couldn't stem the excitement and smiled up at him. He was clean shaven this morning, and as wrapped up as she was, but that didn't stop the pulse of attraction leaping between them. The only difference was this time his smile reached his eyes and they smouldered at her, making her pulse rate soar.

'Yes; are we going to the house you told me about yesterday?'

'We are, yes. The house I spent summers at with my mother and her parents.'

She wanted to ask if his father had gone there too, but didn't dare risk spoiling the softer mood he was in. She sensed his father was the cause of the sudden change in his mood yesterday at his childhood home, but didn't have the courage to ask. Instead she focused her attention on what was happening now. 'Is it far?'

'No, a short car ride, then something special,' he said and to her surprise took her hand and led her into the street to the same big, black car he'd driven the previous day. Her heart fluttered as she fought to control the powerful surge of attraction rushing through her; she'd never felt anything like it before.

Then the something special Nikolai had teased her with turned out to be a ride across the snow in a sleigh, pulled by three proud horses, and Emma was totally blown away by the whole experience—and by the enforced close proximity of Nikolai as they sat snuggled under a heavy throw. 'This is amazing. I can use it in the article.'

'It's called a troika; racing them is a tradition from over one hundred years ago that's enjoying a resurgence.' She could barely focus on what he was saying as his thigh pressed hard against hers and even through all their layers of clothes her skin felt scorched.

After a little while the troika driver slowed to a halt, the horses snorting into the cold air, and Emma looked at Nikolai. Again something fizzed between them, but this time he held her gaze, looking intently into her eyes just the way she would have envisaged a lover doing. 'Thank you,' she whispered softly, her breath hanging briefly in the air, mingling with his in the most intimate way, and making her blush.

'The pleasure is all mine, Emma.' The fact that he'd used her name didn't go unnoticed and a shimmer of pleasure rushed over her, making her shudder, but it wasn't from the cold. 'Are you cold?'

'No, not at all,' she said, shyness creeping over her,

and she lowered her gaze, concentrating on the throw which covered their legs, locking them into the small space together.

With a gloved hand, Nikolai lifted her chin, forcing her to look at him once more, and what she saw in the inky black depths of his eyes was as terrifying as it was exciting. 'You are very beautiful, Emma.'

She swallowed hard, unable to move away from him, trapped with her legs all but welded to his beneath the cover. 'You shouldn't say things like that.'

Was that really her voice? She had no idea she could sound so husky and so trembling at the same time. Deep within her, silly, romantic notions she always shunned sprang to life. Did he really find her attractive? Would he want to kiss her and, if he did, what would it be like?

'It's the truth.'

Her heart was thumping in her chest and she was sure he must hear it. Her breathing had become more rapid, and so had his, if their white, misty breath was anything to go by. She searched his face for any hint of teasing, any sign that he was toying with her. She didn't have any experience with men, but she knew well enough from friends how they could make a woman lose all sense of self, something Richard had never done to her.

There was nothing, not a single trace of him teasing her, and she knew she was in danger of slipping under the spell that the magic of the moment was weaving around them. If they had been in a hotel lounge, talking in front of an open fire as they had done the afternoon she arrived, would he be saying these things to her?

'I didn't come here to become mixed up with a man.'

Even as her body yearned for the unknown, her mind kept to the practical issue of keeping her feet firmly on the ground.

'Do we have to get "mixed up", as you so nicely put it?' His voice was deep and laden with a hidden agenda.

She looked away, across the vast, white expanse of the snowy landscape, and asked herself the same question. If she took the kiss she was sure he wanted to give, would that change anything between them? No, because it couldn't. She had a job to do and then it would be time to move on with her life.

She'd waited in the hope that Richard would move their friendship to something more intimate and now she wondered if that had been wrong. Or was it just Richard who was wrong?

'No, I guess we don't.' She hoped she sounded as though she knew what she was doing, as if she'd been in this very situation many times before. The reality was very different. She'd never had a man look at her with such fierce desire in his eyes, never wanted to feel his lips claim hers.

He responded by moving closer and brushing his lips over hers very gently and suddenly she wasn't cold any more as heat scorched through her. She moved her lips against his, a soft sigh of pleasure slipping from her, only to be caught by him. What was happening to her?

A jolt threw her away from him and she dragged in a long, cold breath as the restless horses shifted in their harnesses. The driver spoke to Nikolai and she blushed, burying her face deeper in her scarf to hide her embarrassment. What was happening to her?

'The driver says snow is on the way and suggests we

see what is necessary and head back.' Nikolai hadn't intended to kiss her like that; he'd just wanted to make her feel special, to give her the fairy-tale ride through the snow to a beautiful location. He'd wanted all that to distract her—at least, he had, until he'd tasted her lips, felt them welcoming him and encouraging him to take more.

'Yes, yes, of course.' She sounded flustered as she took her camera out of its protective case. 'I'll just take a few frames and then you can tell me about it on the way back. I'd rather be in the warm when the snow arrives.'

He pushed back the image of that warmth being his bed and forced himself to focus on the task at hand. He had to distract her from the truth of his family history by showing her the façade they had lived behind.

'This,' he said as he helped her from the troika, 'Is where my mother and I spent each summer until we left Russia. In the summer, though, it was much greener and warmer than now.'

He hadn't thought of those summer days for such a long time, consigning them to the past he wanted to forget, but now, as he began to talk to Emma, it wasn't nearly as hard to look back on them as he'd always feared.

'And this was your mother's family home?' she asked as she lined up the shot and took a photo of the one place he'd been happy as a child.

'It was, but I never saw it like this, all covered in snow. It was always summer when we visited and I'd run with the dogs in the orchard, enjoying the freedom.'

It hadn't been just the freedom of running free in the summer sun, it had been the freedom from the terror of his father: from not having to hide when his filthy temper struck; of not having to worry about his mother as his father's voice rose to aggressive shouts. It had been freedom from pain—for both of them. He'd realised much later on that his mother's parents must have known what was going on and it had been their way of offering sanctuary. He just couldn't understand why his mother hadn't taken it permanently.

'And is your grandmother here to talk to us now?' Hope was shining in her voice. She thought he meant the grandmother who had started this whole nonsense off.

'No, they passed away before my father. Marya Petrushov is my father's mother. The one who contacted *World in Photographs*. She lives in Vladimir.'

'So we can see her?'

She turned her attention to packing away the camera, obviously happy with the photos she'd taken, and he was glad she couldn't see his face—because right now he was sure it must be contorted with rage and contempt for the woman who had done nothing to help him or his mother. Instead she'd preferred to make excuses for her son and for that he could never forgive her.

'Tomorrow. But right now we should return to the hotel.'

Just as he couldn't put off returning to the hotel because of the impending snow, he knew he couldn't put off meeting his grandmother again any longer. Maybe facing her for the first time would be easier with someone else at his side. It might also be the worst possible decision he'd ever made.

CHAPTER THREE

NIKOLAI LOOKED OUT of the window of the hotel bar as darkness descended. The snow was falling ever harder and he couldn't help but feel relieved. At this rate they wouldn't be able to get to his grandmother's home before Emma had to return to London. He'd almost given away the secret himself when he'd taken her to his childhood home; but at least she now had something for her story, and he could relax, maybe even enjoy the evening with her.

'It's snowing really hard.' Emma's voice, soft and gentle, held a hint of anxiety as she joined him in the hotel bar.

'That is normal for these parts,' he said as she sat down, unable to drag his eyes from her. She wore a black dress which moulded to every curve of her body, but when she removed her jacket, exposing her shoulders and slender arms, that spark of attraction he'd been trying to ignore roared forward, more persistent in its need for satisfaction.

She sat down opposite him in the comfortable chairs of the lounge area and crossed her legs, affording him a tantalising view of her lower leg, now deliciously on display, and the black high heels she wore only reinforced his need to feel those legs around him. Was she doing it on purpose? Was she trying to distract him?

'Thank you,' she said firmly and he looked at her face, liking the extra make-up she wore. It accentuated the green of her eyes and he wondered how they would look filled with passion and desire. 'For what you have shown me, I mean. It can't have been easy seeing your childhood home in ruins.'

The sincerity in her voice made him curious about her childhood and he remembered what she'd said within those first moments of meeting him: *life has taught me that, Mr Petrushov.* Had life been equally unkind to her?

'What of your family home?' he asked, instantly recognising the way she tensed and the tightening of her jaw. He wasn't the only one with secrets which still hung over him.

'A family home isn't something I was lucky enough to have. My sister and I were put into care when we were young.' She looked away from him; he watched her swallow down her pain and had to fight hard against the urge to go to her and offer comfort—sure it wouldn't be comfort for long.

'I didn't intend to upset you.' He leant forward in the chair and her perfume weaved itself around him, increasing the desire for her which pumped around his body. Desire he couldn't act on, not if he wanted to keep this whole situation free of complications.

'Maybe it's only fair, after what you endured yesterday. It must have been heart-breaking, seeing your family home like that.' She turned to look at him and suddenly they were very close. He held her gaze, looking into those green eyes and seeing an array of emotions swirling within them. He watched her lips move as she spoke again. 'I feel responsible for that.'

She looked down again at her hands clasped in her lap. For a moment he followed her gaze and then something he'd never experienced before pushed him on. He needed to touch her so he reached out and with his thumb and finger lifted her chin, forcing her to look at him.

The spark of attraction that had been between them from the moment she had got off the train mutated into desire as her gaze locked with his. It arced between them, pulling them together. He pressed the pad of his thumb along her bottom lip and he knew he'd already crossed the line, already passed the point of no return. All he could hope for now was that she would stop this madness from going further. She didn't. She stayed still, her eyes wide and beautiful, and when his fingers caressed her soft skin again her eyes fluttered closed, long lashes spreading out over her pale skin.

Did she have any idea what she was doing to him?

'Maybe we should eat.' Her voice was husky as she looked back up at him, her eyes full of desire. Food was the last thing he wanted, but he couldn't give in to the hot surge of lust racing through him, not when he'd decided this woman was off limits; he'd always prized himself on control.

As she closed her eyes slowly, her lips parting slightly, he wondered how the hell he was supposed to hang on to any sense of decency. She was so alluring, so tempting. When she opened her eyes again the mossy green was swirling with the same lust-filled desire which coursed wildly through his veins and he knew it was too late. There was only one way this heated attraction could be calmed now.

'It is not food I hunger for.' He leant even closer, still holding her chin, and pressed his lips briefly against hers, leaving her in no doubt what it was he hungered for. Was he insane? He'd gone past caring. Somewhere in the recess of his mind he knew this was so wrong, but the thought of kissing her, making her his, was so very right.

Emma could hardly breathe. The message in Nikolai's eyes was so very clear she couldn't miss it. He wanted her. She had no idea how she knew that, having done nothing more than kiss a man. But on a primal level that she'd never known existed within her she recognised the hunger in those inky-black eyes.

Hunger for her.

After years of believing she was unattractive to men, this powerful, dominating man wanted her. Worse than that—she wanted him too. She wanted to taste his kiss and feel his arms around her. She was so far from home, and everything she'd hoped this trip would bring looked in doubt, but right now none of that mattered. Only the searing hot attraction between them mattered. Only the promise of being desired for the woman she was.

What was it her last foster mother had always said? *Live for the moment.* She let the advice swirl in her mind, pushing back the cruel words her father had taunted her with the one and only time she'd met him.

She looked again at Nikolai, at the intensity in his eyes. She'd never done that before, never taken the lead with a man, even though she'd always hoped she and

Richard could be something. Now she knew why. What she felt for him was purely friendship, whereas what she felt for Nikolai, and had done since the moment they'd met, was far more intense. She had no choice but to live for the moment. If she kissed him, allowed herself to step into the sanctuary of his strong arms, would that be living for the moment?

'Neither am I.' Her whisper was so soft she wondered if she'd actually said anything, but the slight rise of his brows and the deepening intensity in his eyes told her she had—and he'd understood.

In answer he lowered his head and covered her lips with his, moving them gently until hers parted, allowing him to deepen the kiss. Heat exploded through her and she knew this was far more than a kiss; this was a prelude to something she'd never done before. He deepened the kiss again, setting light to her whole body. They couldn't do this here. Anyone could see them.

She pulled back, alarmed at how her heart raced, thumping in her chest like a horse galloping across the finishing line. Except this wasn't the end. This was only the beginning. Empowered by that knowledge and the need to let go of restraint and become a real woman, one who knew desire and passion, she smiled at him. 'Let's go upstairs.'

He looked down at her, his eyes searching hers, and she hoped he wouldn't be able to tell how inexperienced she was. A man like this must have had many lovers and the last thing he'd want would be a shy virgin. Although she couldn't change the fact that she'd never done more than kiss a man lightly on the lips, she could stop herself from being shy. All she needed to do was let go and live for the moment.

'It can't be anything more than this night,' he said as he took her hand. 'I don't want a relationship and commitment. I'm not looking for love and happiness. I want to know you understand that, Emma.'

'Love and happiness,' she said, a little too sharply, if his hardening expression was any gauge. 'It doesn't exist, Nikolai. I'm not a fool. In just three days we will go our separate ways and it will be as if this night never happened.'

Where had all that come from? Had passion muddled her mind? She was actually asking to spend the night with him, just one night and nothing more. She who'd told herself she would wait for her Prince Charming, although deep down she knew he didn't exist. Her childhood might have been hard, but it had grounded her expectations of life. She knew true love didn't exist—or, if it did, it never lasted once passion had subsided.

He said nothing. Instead he took her hand in his and led her away from the hotel lounge. Her hand was small in his as she glanced down at it, but she didn't pull back. Her step didn't falter. She was emboldened by the fizz of powerful desire humming in her body, the freedom to be a very different woman and a chance to erase the ever-present doubt her father had planted within her by denying she existed.

As they walked along the corridors of the chalet-style building she wondered if anyone else could tell that she was on fire at the thought of what she was about to do. But there wasn't anyone around and finally he stopped outside his room. She leant against the wall, needing the support of something solid as her knees weakened just from the intensity in his eyes.

'Are you sure this is what you want?' His voice broke as desire turned it into a very sexy whisper. He touched his hand to her face, brushing his fingers down her cheek, but she kept her gaze firmly on him.

Did he think she was playing games? She'd never been as sure of anything in her life. Whatever had ignited between them during those first moments they had met was destined to end like this. There could be no other outcome. Even she knew that and this was exactly what she wanted.

'Yes.' The word came out as a husky whisper and boldly she placed the palms of her hands on his chest, relishing the strength beneath his shirt and cashmere sweater.

His arms wrapped around her, pulling her against him, and a startled gasp slipped from her as she felt the hardness of him pressing intimately against her, awakening her further. To hide her embarrassment she slipped her hands around his neck, her fingers sliding into the dark hair at his collar.

His mouth claimed hers in a demanding kiss, one which stoked the fire he'd lit, sending it roaring higher until she knew it would totally consume her. The dark stubble on his face burned her skin with pleasure. His tongue slid into her mouth, tasting her, teasing her. She matched his kiss, demanding as much from him as he did from her. Whatever this was, she intended to make the most of it. Just for one night she would give in to her own needs and do exactly what she wanted. For one night she was going to put herself first, believe in herself, believe that at least someone cared, someone wanted her.

His hands cupped her bottom, pulling her tighter

against him. His breathing had become as ragged as hers and she plunged her fingers deep into his hair, kissing him harder still. When he broke the kiss she gasped and let her head fall back, her carefully pinned-up hair beginning to fall apart—just as she was.

He kissed down her neck and she arched herself harder against him. She gasped as he kissed lower still over the swell of her breast and right along the neckline of her dress. It wasn't enough. She wanted more, much more.

'Take me to your bed.' Horrified and excited that she'd been bold enough to say what she felt, what she wanted, she laughed. Who was this woman?

'That is exactly what I intend to do, Emma Sanders. You can be sure of that.' Instead of letting her go and opening the door of his room, he kissed her again, one hand holding her back as the other slid up her side and to her breast.

Pleasure exploded around her as his fingers teased her hardened nipple through the fabric of her dress. She couldn't take much more of this. As if he read her thoughts, he pulled back and let her go. She stood and watched as he unlocked the room and pushed the door open. Was she really doing this? Was she really about to step into this man's room and give herself to him?

Embarrassment rushed over her again, but she hid it with boldness, walking towards him with a suggestive smile on her lips. Tonight she wasn't Emma Sanders, responsible for everyone else, she was just a woman drowning in desire. With a gentleness which surprised her after the kiss that had bruised her lips, he took her hand and led her into the room. Quietly he clicked the door shut and they were left in almost darkness, the only light coming from outside, creeping in through the blinds in beams of whiteness.

Nikolai looked at Emma, not wanting to turn the lights on, but wanting to see how beautiful she was. In one minute she seemed bold and seductive and then, as if a switch had been flicked, she looked innocent and shy. He had no idea which was the real Emma, but either way she was full of passion and desire. More importantly she shared his views. Love and happiness were only for the select few and they were not destined to be two of those.

'You are very beautiful,' he said as he moved towards her. Those expressive green eyes widened, pushing the desire within him higher still. He'd never wanted a woman as much as he wanted her and for that very reason he intended to savour every moment. Was it because she didn't threaten him by hinting at beyond the here and now, looking for more than just one night? Or was it because they had both known pain and hardship in their lives? Either way, he wasn't going to rush one minute of their night together, not when it was all they had.

'Nikolai…' She breathed his name, a hint of a question lingering in her whisper.

'Now is not for talking,' he said gently, pulling her to him. 'It's for pleasure like this.'

Before she could say anything else, he kissed her, resisting the urge to deepen the kiss and demand so much more. Savour the moment. Those words played in his mind as her lips parted beneath his, her tongue tentatively entwining with his.

With practised ease, his fingers found the zip at the

back of her dress and pulled it slowly down her back as she deepened the kiss. He pulled back from her, needing a moment to gather his control again. Her lips were parted and her eyes so full of desire they were almost closed.

He took the straps of her dress and slid them slowly off her shoulders and down her arms. The only movement was the rise and fall of her delectable breasts as she breathed deeply. He let the straps go as his hands lowered past her elbows and the dress slithered to the floor, leaving her in a black bra and panties.

Her eyes had widened and she looked at him, the innocent woman who'd slipped in and out of the limelight back once more. Then she smiled and the innocence was gone, the bold temptress returning as she reached behind and unfastened her bra, letting it fall away to expose full breasts, testing his control further. Then slowly, without breaking eye contact, she pulled her panties lower, wriggling with ease out of the black lace. Finally she stood and looked at him, a challenge in her mischievous smile. Was she daring him to resist her or daring him to make her his for tonight?

'You are even more beautiful now… I want to taste every part of you.' Just saying those words made his pulse leap with heated desire, but when she stepped towards him, her naked body highlighted by the pale light from outside, it was almost too much.

'I want you to.' She reached up and stroked the backs of her fingers over his stubble. It was such an erotic sensation he was glad he was still fully clothed, otherwise he would have pushed her back on the bed and plunged into her; all thought of making the pleasure last would have gone.

He caught her wrist, putting a stop to her caress before it pushed him over the edge. She looked up at him and for a second he thought he saw shock, but she recovered before he could analyse it, pressing her naked body against him wickedly. He let her wrist go and trailed his fingers down her arm and then to her breast, circling the tight bud of her nipple. She wasn't the only one who could be so wickedly teasing.

'And so I shall,' he said and lowered his head to tease her nipple with his tongue. She pushed her hands into his hair as he moved to her other breast to begin the torment again. Then he dropped to his knees and kissed down her stomach, holding her hips tightly as a spike of lust threatened his control. Gently he moved lower, teasing at the dark curls as she gasped her pleasure and gripped her hands tightly in his hair.

'I never knew,' she gasped, writhing beneath his exploration, 'that it could be so nice, so…'

'You make is sound like you've never made love.' He looked up at her, each breath she took making him want her all the more.

'Would that be so bad?' She looked at him and bit at her lower lip. He frowned in confusion, wondering if this was why one minute she was a temptress, the next an innocent. Was she telling him she was inexperienced—or even a virgin? After the moments they'd just shared, and her boldness, could that really be true?

'Why do you ask?'

'It's just that I've never…I'm a…' She blushed, unable to finish the sentence, the temptress gone.

'You are a virgin?' Shock rocked through him, followed by something else. She'd never made love and was choosing him to be her first lover.

'Yes,' she whispered and looked down at him, her eyes full of longing. 'And I want you to be the man who shows me what desire and passion is like.'

He stood up and took her hands in his, looking at her as she stood naked before him, uncertainty all over her beautiful face. He shouldn't want her, shouldn't want to be the man who showed her the pleasures of sex for the first time, but an overwhelming need to be that man flowed through him, making him want her more, testing his control beyond endurance.

'It wouldn't change anything, Emma.' He wanted her to be sure, wanted her to know that after this there wasn't anything else. 'If we have sex it will still be just tonight. I don't want a relationship. I don't intend to settle down any time soon.'

She pressed her palm against his face, her fingers running over the stubble, unleashing the same wild desire as before. 'I want nothing more than this moment in time.'

He pulled her to him, enjoying her soft skin beneath his hands and the feel of her nakedness against his clothed body. He kissed her gently, determined to make this as special as possible—for both of them.

In one swift movement he swept her up in his arms and carried her to the large bed he'd spent the last two nights alone in. As he placed her on the soft covers, he allowed his fingers to trail over her, his gaze fixed firmly on hers.

He stood before her and pulled off his clothes, enjoying the way she watched, her eyes widening when he stood before her naked and aroused. He picked up his wallet from the bedside table and pulled out the all-important foil packet. 'I assume this is the only contraception we have between us?'

The impish smile which had been on her face as she'd watched him divest himself of his clothes slipped away as he rolled the condom on. 'It is, yes.'

He moved on to the bed, bracing his arms on either side of her head, his body tantalisingly close to her as he teased her with a kiss. 'Now that we've sorted that out, we can get back to the important issue of pleasure.'

She wrapped her arms around his neck, pulling him to her, and he had to fight hard to stop himself covering that delicious body with his and thrusting into her. As she stroked her fingers down his back, returning his kiss with ever more passion, he knew he couldn't hold out much longer and he moved on top of her. She wrapped her legs around him; if he hadn't known she was a virgin, he'd never have considered it possible, as she rocked her hips teasing him mercilessly.

His control snapped and all he could think about was making her his. She gasped out and dug her fingernails into his back as he took possession of her, sliding in as gently as his burning need for her allowed. She opened her eyes and looked up at him as he moved within her.

'Nikolai…' She whispered his name and moved her hips with him, encouraging him to deepen that possession and pushing him over the edge.

He reached that edge, trying to hang on, trying to take her with him, and when she met him there he finally let go, collapsing afterwards into her embrace, their breathing hard and fast.

CHAPTER FOUR

IT WAS STILL dark when Emma awoke, her body humming from the exquisite pleasure of making love with Nikolai. Movement caught her attention and she looked towards the window where the soft light of dawn was starting to creep around the blinds. Nikolai stood looking out through the blinds, his body partially in shadow and every sculpted muscle of his torso highlighted like a black-and-white photo. He'd pulled on a pair of jeans and in her mind Emma filed the image away as if she'd pressed the button on her camera and taken it.

His forehead was close to the blinds as he stood looking out. He was completely lost in thought and didn't hear the soft rustle of the bedclothes as she sat up. His jaw was tense and his brow furrowed into a frown. What was he thinking? Was he angry that she wasn't the experienced seductress she'd tried so hard to be? Had their one night been disappointing for him?

'Is it still snowing?' she asked as she propped herself up on her elbow, needing to say something to break the heavy silence around them. She hoped it was snowing too much for them to do what he'd planned today and, if it was, would he come back to bed?

She'd never expected to find what she had discov-

ered last night in his arms, that completeness, as if
they belonged together. The romantic inside her that
she always tried hard to supress wanted more, so much
more, but the ever-present realist that life had made her
pushed those silly notions aside. Once she left Vladimir, there could be no more. This was just a fling for
him, a way to amuse himself on a cold snowy night.
It could even be a way to distract her from what she'd
come here to do. That thought slipped uncomfortably
over her but she refused to give it any importance; after
all hadn't there been an undeniable spark of attraction
between them since the moment she'd arrived?

Nikolai continued to look out at the snow, as if he
hadn't heard her, and just when she thought she might
have to ask again he turned and looked at her, lines of
worry creasing his brow. 'It is.'

The roughness of his voice made her swallow hard
against the disappointment which rushed through her.
What had she expected? A declaration of undying love
because she'd given him her virginity? Even she knew
better than that!

'Will it stop us meeting your grandmother?' She
tried hard to keep her voice soft and calm, as if discuss-
ing the weather with the man she'd just had the most
wonderful sex with was as normal as the snow falling
over the Russian landscape in winter.

He turned to look at her, so slowly she wondered if
she'd said something really wrong. With casual ease he
hooked his thumb in the belt loop of his jeans and fixed
her with a deep and penetrating gaze, and the unmistakable stamp of suspicion was on his handsome face.

'Would that be a problem?'

It should be but Emma realised with shock that it

wouldn't be, not if she could stay cocooned here with Nikolai and lose herself in a moment she hadn't expected at all. A moment which had unlocked a passionate woman within her she'd never known existed, a woman she wanted to be again before the coldness of daybreak brought reality back.

'No,' she whispered softly. 'Let's not think of anything else until daylight.'

Her words lifted the tension which had folded around them, but as he stepped towards her, every muscle highlighted for her pleasure by the growing light from outside, that tension was replaced with something far more powerful.

'Looking at you right now, that is exactly what I want to do.'

Emma pulled aside the tousled sheets, inviting him back into bed, and as he pulled off his jeans and slipped in beside her she was in no doubt what he wanted to do. Heat uncoiled deep within her, lighting the flame of desire once more. Never in her wildest dreams had she expected to find this when she'd boarded the plane for Moscow and she knew that it would change her life for ever.

'I want to be yours til morning breaks,' she said as she moved against the heat of his body, relishing the strength of his arms around her as he pressed her into the bed, covering her body with his, passion exploding like fireworks around them.

'Until daylight,' he said as he kissed her lips, then made a blazing trail down her throat. 'You will be mine, Emma.'

Nikolai felt his control slip away as he pushed the reality of the world aside and kissed Emma. How could she make him feel like this—so lost unless he was holding her, kissing her, as if she truly was his? Her hands moved over his body and her warm skin pressed close against his and all he could think was that she was his, totally his.

The fire of desire ripped through him as her lips claimed his, demanding so much and giving even more. It was so wild, so intense, all he could think about was making her his. Nothing else mattered but that. All he wanted was to be deep inside her.

'Nikolai!' She gasped his name and arched herself up to meet him as he claimed her once more, a powerful urge almost totally consuming him. 'Don't forget…'

A curse flew from him as he pulled back from her and the release which threatened to come far too quickly. How could one woman obliterate his control? Undo him so completely? Feeling like a fumbling teenager, he dealt with the contraception as she looked up at him, desire-darkened eyes holding his.

'This time there is nothing to stop us.' His words were smothered as her lips claimed his and her body welcomed him, taking him deep within her.

An explosion of heated emotions erupted, making him shudder as his release came hard and fast. He kissed Emma, binding them ever closer as the same wave he was riding crashed over her. The sea of desire left him swirling in exhaustion and, as her hold on him turned to a soft caress of his back, he allowed himself to slip under, to give in to the pleasure of sleeping in a woman's arms in a way he'd never done before.

When he woke several hours later, Emma's body warm against his, he didn't want to move, didn't want to give up the moment. Never before had he allowed emotion into the bedroom. For him it had always been about lust and acting upon an attraction. He'd thought it would be the same with Emma when he'd taken her to his room, but the moment he'd taken her virginity, had become her only lover, something had changed.

Gently he kissed her hair as she lay against his chest. Immediately she lifted her head and looked at him, a shy smile on her face. 'You could always just tell me about your family and then we can stay here all day instead of going to see your grandmother.'

His mood was lighter than it had ever been and he stroked his hands through the softness of her hair. 'If I tell you too much, I will have to keep you here for ever.'

'Promises, promises.' She laughed, a soft, sexy laugh which pushed him further from reality.

'You know the basics,' he said as she kissed his chest, forcing him to close his eyes. 'I grew up in Russia and when my father died my mother and I left for New York.'

'That must have been tough.' Her slender fingers traced across his chest, easing the pain of the memories, the pain of telling them.

'My mother had help from a business acquaintance of my father's and, several years later, she married him.' The surprised rise of her brows made him think more deeply and the hum of passion dimmed.

'Did you mind? That she married again, I mean, replaced your father?' If there was one question sure to kill the desire which had rampaged through him, it was that one.

'I didn't mourn my father.' The pain from his childhood made his voice a harsh growl and Emma pulled away from him to look up into his face. Could she sense the tension in him just thinking about how he'd been conceived, that he had been the product of a violent rape?

'What happened?' There wasn't any disgust in her voice for his open admission, no judgement in those two words at all. Had she too known childhood heartache? Did she recognise it within him?

'It was not a happy marriage and one my grandmother, Marya Petrushov, very much wanted to continue. She made things difficult for my mother, prolonged the unhappiness.' He skirted around the truth, trying to explain without giving her any more of the sorry secret than she needed to know. She could even be storing away the information right now to put it in her damned article. He pulled away from her, broke the contact. It was the only way to be able to think straight.

'Is that why you have been distracting me from meeting her?' The bold question didn't match the soft innocence of the image she created naked in his bed and he fought hard against the urge to abandon this conversation and use the language of desire and passion. Her next words killed that thought, so instantly his body froze. 'I need the story, Nikolai, all of it. I have a job to do.'

How could she look so deliciously sexy when her words were like hail thrashing his naked body? Had he fallen for the oldest trick in the book? Had she acted innocent to ensure he took her to his bed and he was now spoiling her plans? Worse than that, had she bargained her virginity just to get the story she needed? He shouldn't be telling her the intimate secrets of his family, not when she could portray a family ripped apart by greed and power as it had risen to new heights of wealth.

It was precisely what had happened. His mother must have been an easy target for a power-hungry man whose own family had come from nothing. Bile rose in his throat at the thought of his father's mother selling the story. Did she expect it to keep her comfortable in her final years? Was she planning even now to blackmail him? It damn well wouldn't happen if he had anything to do with it.

'You'll get your story,' he growled as he stood up and stepped away from her, away from the temptation of her silky, soft skin. She was as devious as his grandmother. She'd only slept with him to get what she wanted. She'd crossed the barriers he'd long ago erected and had exposed his emotions to the light of a new day and, with it, the pain of who he was. 'But not now. Not until I know if there are consequences from your underhanded way of interviewing me.'

'Nikolai!' she gasped and reached out, the sheet slipping, giving a tantalising view of her breasts. The fact that it turned him on, sending lust hurtling through him faster than anything he'd known, disgusted him.

He turned his back on her, not trusting himself to leave her alone, and savagely pulled on the remainder of his clothes. He'd been a fool. He'd thought he'd glimpsed what life could be like if his past wasn't a permanent shadow hanging over him.

'You need to leave.' He turned to look at her, allowing the anger to sluice over him and wash away the lingering desire. She was as deceitful and scheming as his grandmother and he wouldn't allow her to expose the truth and hurt his mother. She'd suffered enough shame.

* * *

Emma blinked and recoiled at the change in Nikolai. Where had the tender lover gone? Anger rushed from him like a fierce tide crashing onto the rocky shore.

'No, we need to talk.'

'I'm not saying anything else to you.' He spat the words back at her, the dim light of the room only making his anger even clearer. What had she done to make him suddenly hate her? The questions had only been part of her job and she'd never hidden that from him.

He stepped closer to her and she became aware of her nakedness again, clutching the covers against her once more. From the hard expression set on his face, she knew their moment of intimacy was over. The connection between them they'd shared last night had been severed as surely as if he'd cut it.

He reached into his jacket pocket and seconds later tossed a business card onto the bed. 'If you want to pry into my life any more, you can contact me on that number.'

Ice shuttered around her heart, freezing the new emotions she'd allowed herself to have for this man. How had she been stupid enough to believe he was different, that like her he was hurting because of the past? She'd thought that made what they'd shared last night more intense, more powerful.

She took the card, holding it as if it might explode at any second. The bold black print in which *Nikolai Cunningham* was written was as hard as the man who stood angrily before her.

'One last thing,' she said before she could think better of it. 'Why do you no longer use your family name, Petrushov?' It was the one thing which had puzzled her since she'd been given the assignment on the Petrushov family and had been told the only grandson would meet her in Vladimir.

'I have no wish to use my father's name.' The harshness in his tone made his hatred and anger palpable. It filled the room and invaded every corner. 'And, so that you have your information correct when you use my family's sordid past to further your career, I changed my name to that of my stepfather when I was sixteen.'

'I'm not going to use any of what you've just told me, Nikolai. What kind of woman do you think I am?' She couldn't keep the shock from her voice or the hurt from cutting deep into her. Did he really think that badly of her?

'You are obviously the kind of woman who will trade her virginity to climb a career ladder.' The hardened growl of his accusation sliced painfully into her, sullying the memories of giving herself to him so completely last night.

'No,' she gasped, wishing she was wearing something so that she could go to him. How could he think that of her? 'It wasn't like that at all.'

He gave her one last frosty glare and then strode to the door. 'Now you have all you need to ruin mine and my mother's reputations, you can get the hell out of my life.'

The door slammed behind him and she was left, blinking in shock. Only hours ago they had been locked in the arms of passion. Nothing else had existed. A tear slid down her face as she threw back the covers and picked up the black dress from the floor, trying not to remember the burn of desire she'd had for him as it had slipped off her body last night. Angrily she pulled it on, not caring about her underwear. All she wanted was to get along the hotel corridor to the sanctuary of her room and lock herself in until her heart stopped breaking.

Still reeling from the shock of Nikolai walking out on her, she shut the door of her own room and made for the shower, needing the warmth of the water to soothe her. After standing there for what felt like hours, Emma finally turned the water off and wrapped herself in a towel, trying not to dwell on the accusations Nikolai had hurled at her. Did he really think she'd all but sold herself just to get information out of him?

Her phone buzzed on the cabinet next to her bed. Instantly she was on alert. What if it was Nikolai? With a slight tremor in her hands she reached for it and, as she looked at the text from her sister, she knew the day was going from bad to worse. Even with the limited words of the text Emma could sense Jess's distress, but it was the final word which really propelled her into motion:

I need you, Em, come now. Please.

Finally the overnight train arrived in Perm and Emma made her way straight to the ballet school. The tearful conversation she'd had with Jess during that long journey was still fresh in her mind, which at least had given her little time to think of the night spent with Nikolai and how it had drastically changed things, how he'd rejected her.

'I've missed you so much, Em,' Jess said, dragging her mind back from thoughts of the tall, dark-haired Russian who had lured the woman she'd always wanted to be out of the shadows.

'Is that what this is all about?' Emma kept her tone light but, for the first time ever, felt constrained by looking after her sister. If she hadn't had to rush and get a train ticket sorted, she might have seen Nikolai again. She'd at least wanted to try and explain, especially after the intimacies they'd shared. All she knew was that he'd checked out.

'You've been so far away and it's been months since I've seen you. I guess I couldn't stand the thought of you being so close.'

'Not exactly close.' Emma forced herself to forget her problems and laughed, pulling her sister into a hug, unable to be irritated by the intrusion into her life at the worst possible moment. 'It was a very long train journey from Vladimir. It took me all night.'

'I hope I didn't spoil anything for you,' said Jess, looking a little subdued suddenly, and Emma wondered if there was more to this.

'There wasn't anything to spoil.' Nikolai had already done that, accusing her of all but seducing the story out of him. Well, she'd show him. Nothing he'd said to her in his room would find its way into her article, although it did go some way to explaining his shock at seeing his family home again.

'That's all right, then,' began Jess, sounding brighter already. 'I only have the rest of today off class, then it's back to it.'

'Then we need to do something really good.'

Later that night, lying alone in a different hotel room, having spent the entire day with Jess, Emma's doubts crept back in. She remembered Nikolai standing at the window, the light shadowing his body, and wished she could turn back time. The only thing she wanted to change was the doubt on his face, the worry in his eyes.

Several times this evening she'd wanted to call him, wanted to reassure him that all he'd told her about his childhood would stay with her. She knew what it was to feel unloved and out of place. Was that why he'd gone to great lengths to put off the meeting with his grandmother? Was there another side to the story? Had she been fooled by his heart-wrenching admission of his past?

She had spent time on the train drafting out what she wanted to write and none of it would include the torture of the man who'd shown her what being loved could be like, even for a few brief hours. If she told him that, would he believe her? She relived the moment he'd accused her of seducing him for information and knew he would never believe her.

Tomorrow she would be taking the train back to Moscow and from there a flight home to London. There wouldn't be an opportunity to see him; maybe fate was trying to tell her that what she'd shared with Nikolai that night was nothing more than a moment out of time.

CHAPTER FIVE

NIKOLAI STOOD AT a window of his apartment, looking at, but not seeing, Central Park bathed in spring sunshine. All he could think about was Emma. It had been almost two months since that night but the only communication had been from *World in Photographs*, thanking him, although he was yet to see a copy of what Emma had submitted. That, however, was the least of his worries.

He'd replayed their night together many times in his mind and, once the anger that she'd slept with him to get her story had cooled, a new worry grew from an inkling of doubt. The more he thought of it, the more his gut was telling him they might have had an accident after she'd coaxed him back to bed...the hurried and last-minute use of the condom playing heavily on his mind.

As he stood looking out of the window early that morning, he kept telling himself that no news from Emma was good, that their night of passion hadn't had the consequences he'd dreaded despite the ever-increasing doubt in his mind.

It had been many weeks since he'd marched from the hotel room and braced the snow to cool his mind and body with a walk. When he'd returned to the room, Emma had gone, and that had told him all he needed to know: he'd been used. The only good thing to come out of the night was that he hadn't had to face his grandmother.

Angry that he'd put himself in such a position, he'd checked out and headed straight back to New York, but he hadn't stopped thinking about Emma. She had haunted his every waking hour and made sleep almost impossible. Something had happened to him that night, maybe even from the first moment he'd met her. She had changed him, made him think of things he couldn't have.

He'd done what he always did where emotions were concerned and avoided them. He still couldn't believe he'd almost told her all about his childhood. Those hours spent in bed with her must have muddled his mind. It should have just been a night of passion to divert her from the horrible truth of who he really was, but he'd almost told her exactly what he'd wanted to remain a secret.

He'd gone to Vladimir and confronted the ghosts of his past in order to save his mother the heartache of seeing her story all over the newspapers, exactly where it would end up once it was published by *World in Photographs*. What he'd found in Vladimir with Emma was something different.

Yes, he had been guilty of wanting to distract her from the truth, but somewhere along the way things had changed. She'd reached into the cold darkness of his heart and unlocked emotions he'd thought impossible to feel. Even the woman he'd once proposed to had failed to do that, but Emma had been different.

'What the hell were you thinking?' He snarled angrily at himself. One of the only times he'd let a woman close and she'd cheated him, used him for her own gain. He'd even begun to question if Emma was as innocent as she'd claimed. Had that too been part of the plan—to make him think he was the first man she'd ever slept with—in order to get the real story?

The fact that she'd run out on him only added fuel to the fire. Not only that, there hadn't been a word from her since that night when he'd stood there and looked at her, clutching the sheet against her. He'd had had to fight hard not to pull the damn thing from her and get back into bed. His body had been on fire with need for her and, despite having spent all night having sex, he'd allowed the anger he felt at himself for being used to have precedence. It had been a far more reliable emotion to feel, one which had propelled him from the hotel room without a backward glance.

Driven by that anger, he'd left quickly, tossing her a card as an afterthought. Or was it because even then, deep down, he knew things might have gone wrong? If their night together did have consequences, then he knew he would face up to them and be the father he'd always longed for in place of the cruel man who had filled his childhood with fear.

The fact that he knew what he would do didn't make Emma's silence any easier. It irritated him. Did it mean she wasn't pregnant? That the condom failure about which he'd since convinced himself hadn't had any drastic consequences?

He looked at his watch. Ten in the morning here meant late afternoon in London. He could ring her. It would be easy enough to get her number through *World in Photographs*, but what would he say?

He'd replayed again the scene in the hotel room early that morning. He'd woken to find her sleeping soundly next to him and had watched her for a while. Then, as the ghosts of the past had crowded in, he'd had to get up. For what had felt like hours, he'd stood watching the dark and empty street outside the window as if it held the answer or truth about his past.

Emma had stirred, her glorious naked body doing things to his, and he'd had to hold on to his self-control, wanting only to lose himself in her once more instead of facing the truth. That truth was not only the fact that she'd lured him to tell her things he'd wanted to keep well hidden.

His phone bleeped, alerting him to a text, and he ignored it, wanting to focus on what to do next. Call her? Go to London and demand to see her? He'd have to find out where she lived.

Insistently the alert sounded again and he swore in Russian, something he hadn't done for a long time before he'd returned to Vladimir. When he picked up the phone and read the text, he almost dropped it as if it were red-hot.

We need to meet. I'm in New York. E

He inhaled deeply. This could only mean one thing—the very worst thing. There was no way she'd come here, all the way to New York, to tell him the article had been accepted, or show him a copy. An email would be sufficient for that. She needed to talk. His suspicions about their night together must be right—she was pregnant with his child—and that changed everything.

He pressed his thumb and finger against his eyelids in an effort to think, but there was only one answer. The same answer that had come up each and every time he'd thought of Emma and that night together. The very thing he'd never wanted to happen. He just knew it: he'd fathered a child. Now he had to face his fears from childhood and prove to himself he wasn't his father's son…that he could bring up his child with love and kindness. The very idea terrified him.

Emma was late. She'd arrived at Central Park early and wandered around taking photographs until midday, the time specified by Nikolai in his reply to her text. She'd tried to put her reason for being in New York to the back of her mind and had almost succeeded when she had become engrossed in taking shots of the park. Now the impending meeting with him loomed large but she couldn't recall which way she'd come. She looked around at the tall buildings surrounding the park and wondered if she'd be able to find her way back out. She was tired from travelling and early pregnancy was not being so kind to her. Panic rose up. She'd have to ask someone for directions.

'Excuse me, is it this way to The Boathouse?' she asked a mother pushing a pram, trying hard not to look down at the child. It would be too much like looking into her future and she wondered how she was ever going to cope on her own. Nikolai had made it more than clear that what they'd shared was just one night. He'd been so adamant about it she began to question her reasons for telling him personally. It would have been much easier just to call him, tell him he was going to be a father. It was her conscience and knowing what it felt like to be rejected by her father that had made her come.

All through the flight one question kept going round in her head: would her own father have wanted to be part of her life if he'd been given the choice like this? The day she'd first met him, after she'd begged her mother to tell her who he was, rushed back at her, as did his icy words. *It's too late. I don't need or want you in my life.*

'Keep walking and you'll see it.' The mother's voice dragged her back to the present. She smiled at Emma before heading on in the other direction. With unease in her heart Emma watched her walk out of sight. That would be her by the end of the year, but she was certain she wouldn't be here in New York, looking happy with life.

She shook the thought away and looked at her watch again. She was fifteen minutes late. Would Nikolai still be there? With the pain of her father's rejection stinging her heart, the need to see Nikolai, to tell him and give him the chance to be part of his child's life, deepened. She quickened her step but within a few strides they faltered. He was standing where the path turned through the trees and, despite the distance, she knew it was him, as if her body had registered his, known he was close.

She could also tell from his stance that he was not happy about being kept waiting. She breathed in deeply, then let the breath out in a bid to calm her nerves and quell the nausea which threatened to rear its head yet again. Within days of returning to London she had woken each morning feeling ill and had at first put it down to all that had happened between her and Nikolai. After all, losing your virginity to a man, only to have him walk out in anger, was not the best experience in the world. Not once had she considered there was a lasting legacy of that night.

As days had turned into a week, she'd known she couldn't ignore the encroaching doubt any longer and had purchased a pregnancy test. The fact that it had taken several more days before she'd been brave enough to use it only served to increase the weight of dread which filled her from the moment she woke each day. When she'd finally had enough courage to use the test, her worry had increased as the ominous blue lines appeared, confirming that the hours spent with Nikolai had most definitely had consequences— for her, at least.

She walked towards him now and with purpose pushed those long, lonely weeks aside in her mind, focusing instead on what had to be done. She kept her chin lifted and her eyes on him all the time. Anything else would be to show uncertainty or, at worst, fear. She wasn't scared of her future any more and, although it was going to be a struggle, she was looking forward to giving her child all she'd never had. What she did fear was telling Nikolai and, from the rigid set of his shoulders, she'd been right to fear this moment.

He made no move towards her, not even one step, and she hated him for doing that. He could have made the moment easier for her. Was he punishing her for contacting him? For making their one night something more? Each step she took must have shown her anxiety a little bit more. She should have called him as soon as she'd taken the pregnancy test, but shock had set in. She hadn't even been ready to accept it herself, let alone blithely call him up and tell him their one night had created a child which would join them for ever.

How did you tell a man who'd made it blatantly clear he didn't want any kind of commitment that he was a father? Her mother obviously hadn't done it right, but could she? She was about to find out.

As she drew level with him, the inky black of his eyes held accusation, just as they had done in the hotel room the morning after they'd spent the night together, the night she'd lost her virginity to him. The firm line of his lips looked harder than they had that morning but she refused to be intimidated, just as she refused to acknowledge the hum of attraction rushing through her just from seeing him, being near him again.

She couldn't still want him; she just couldn't.

'You are late.' He snapped the words out and stood his ground. Six foot plus of brooding male towered over her, sending her heartbeat racing in a way that had nothing to do with nerves at what she had to say. She hated the way she still wanted him, her body in complete denial of the numbness in her mind. How could she still want a man who'd rejected her so coldly after she'd given him her most precious gift?

'I couldn't find my way through the park…' she began, trying to instil firmness into her voice, but he cruelly cut her off.

'Why are you here, Emma?' The hard glint in his eye sparked with anger but she wouldn't allow him to make her feel like a guilty child. What right did he have to stand there and dictate to her what she should have done and when? He was the one who'd strode from the hotel room in Vladimir without a word to her after tossing her his card. He was the one who hadn't handled this right.

'Did you think throwing a business card onto the bed was a nice way to end our night together?' Her words spiked the spring air around them, but he didn't flinch. His handsome face didn't show a single trace of any other emotion beyond controlled annoyance. This just prodded at her anger, firing her up. 'We need to talk, Nikolai. That's why I'm here.'

'About the consequences of our night together?' He'd guessed. Guilt and shock mixed together and she looked up at him, not yet able to say anything.

He moved towards her, dominating the spring air around them, and while she heard people walking past she couldn't do anything other than focus on him. If she looked away, even for just a second, all her strength would slip away.

'By consequences, you mean pregnancy.' Finally she found her voice. Her sharp words didn't make a dent in his assured superiority, but saying them aloud filled her with panic.

'Yes, exactly that. I assume you haven't flown halfway around the world to tell me about the article. You're here to tell me you are expecting my child.' He looked straight into her eyes, the fierce question in them mixing with accusation. Was he blaming her?

Emma looked away from the impenetrable hardness in his eyes and wished it could be different, but no amount of wishing was going to change those two bold lines on the pregnancy test she'd finally had the courage to use. She was pregnant with Nikolai's child and, judging by his response to her arrival in New

York, he did not like that particular revelation. It didn't matter what he said now, she had to face the truth: she was very much alone.

She let out a soft breath, trying to come to terms with what she'd known all along, finally accepting why she'd wanted to tell him in person. She'd had the faint hope that he would come around to the idea, be different from her father. But no. If the fierce glint in his cold black eyes was anything to go by, he didn't want to be a father at any price. She would do this herself. She didn't need him—or anyone. 'Your powers of deduction are enviable, Nikolai. Yes, I'm pregnant.'

Nikolai braced himself against the worst possible news he could ever be told. He couldn't be a father, not when the example he'd seen of fatherly love still haunted his dreams, turning them into nightmares if he allowed it.

He looked at Emma, the one woman who'd captured a part of his heart. Ever since she'd left he'd tried to tell himself it was because he'd shared a bit of himself with her, shared secrets he hadn't wanted anyone to know. He still couldn't comprehend why he'd done that when she'd had the power to make it completely public, shatter his mother's peaceful life and destroy his hard-won business reputation. He was thankful he'd stopped at the unhappy marriage bit, glad he hadn't told her the full horror of how that marriage had come about. How he'd come about. If she knew the truth she wouldn't want him to have anything to do with his child, of that he was sure. But, although he had shared some secrets, he would now do anything he could to ensure those she didn't know about stayed hidden away.

'And did you leave Vladimir in such a hurry because

you thought you'd discovered extra facts for the story? Perhaps you rushed off to get it in?'

The anger he'd felt when he'd realised she'd left not only his room and the hotel but Vladimir itself still coursed through him. He'd had to leave her in the hotel room because of the desire coursing through him. He'd needed the cool air to dull the heavy lust she evoked in him with every look. He hadn't intended it to be the last time he saw her. He'd intended to go back and talk calmly with her, hear what she would want if the worst had indeed happened.

'No.' She looked down, as he quickly realised she always did when confronted with something difficult, as if she too was hiding from past hurt— or was it guilt for throwing herself at him just to get a few snippets of inside information? When she looked back up at him, her eyes were shining with threatening tears. 'I had a call from my sister and left soon after you did.'

'A call from your sister? So, after we'd worked together on the article, you thought spending time with her was more important?' Her face paled at his icy tone and a rush of guilt sliced briefly through him before he pushed it aside. She'd run out on him to play happy families with her sister.

'She was upset.' Emma looked up at him as if imploring him to understand. 'We only have each other. I left her to go back to Moscow but there wasn't any time to contact you again. It's not as if I knew there were such consequences then.'

'When did you first discover these consequences?' The fact that she must have known for at least a few weeks infuriated him more than the fact that she'd used

him, seduced him into taking her to bed and spilling
secrets.

'I've only fairly recently had it confirmed...' He
moved even closer to her, dominating the very air she
breathed and halting her words in mid-flow.

'And now we have to deal with it.' His attention was
caught by passers-by, happy in the spring sunshine
when he now had the weight of guilt pressing down
on him, all but rooting him to the spot like one of the
large trees of the park.

This was his fault. He should have been more care-
ful, more in control, but if he was honest with himself
he should never have given in to the attraction in the
first place. Not with the woman who had the power to
destroy his and his mother's happiness. What the hell
had he been thinking? What had happened to his usual
self-control? Emma had happened. She'd completely
disarmed him, which he strongly suspected had been
her intention all along.

'Deal with it?' He heard the panic in her voice and
turned his attention back to her, to see she'd paled
even more dramatically. She needed to sit down. He
did too, but the restaurant would be busy, far too busy
to discuss an unplanned pregnancy and the ramifica-
tions of such news.

'This way,' he said as he took her arm, ensuring she
came with him. He strode towards the edge of the park
where he knew the horse-drawn carriages would be
waiting for customers. They could talk as they toured
the park and, more importantly, she wouldn't be able
to run out on him this time. She would have to face
their situation, just as he'd had to as he'd gone over
this very moment in his mind during recent weeks. In

the carriage she would have no choice but to listen to him and accept that his solution was their only option.

'Where are we going?' She pulled back against him as if she was on the verge of bolting again, backing up his reasoning for taking a carriage ride like a tourist.

'Somewhere we can talk. Somewhere you'll have no choice but to sit and hear what I have to say, how we are going to deal with this.' Still she resisted and he turned to face her, sliding his hand down her arm to take her hand in his. As he did so, that fizz of energy filled him once more and he could see her face again, full of desire the night she'd taken his hand in Vladimir. The night they'd conceived a new life. His child. His heir. 'You are not going to slip away so easily this time, Emma, not now you carry my child.'

The determination and bravado slipped from Emma and her body became numb. She was too tired to fight any more, too tired to worry and fret over the future, and Nikolai's suggestion of sitting down seemed the best option. She walked hand in hand with him through the park. To onlookers they would have appeared like any other couple, walking together in the sunshine, but inside dread had begun to fill her, taking over the sizzle of attraction from just being with him again. Exactly how did he intend to deal with it?

'We'll take a ride round the park,' Nikolai said as he stopped beside a horse-drawn carriage and she blinked in shock. Was this just another of his romantic pastimes to distract her? Then the truth of that thought hit her. That was exactly what he'd done in Vladimir. He'd gone out of his way to distract her and had even successfully managed to keep her from meeting his grandmother.

He'd been keeping her from knowing more about his family and, thinking back to the moment they'd met, she could see he'd been evasive about the story of rags to riches she was supposed to cover. Why, then, had he said the things he had that morning after they'd made love, giving her a deeper insight into the childhood which had shaped the man he now was?

She still couldn't shake off the sensation that he'd wanted to say more but had guarded against it. Had he really believed she would put all those details in the article? She'd just wanted to create a fairy-tale story to go with the amazing photographs she'd taken, but he'd accused her of manipulating everything to get what she wanted.

'Trying to make me all soft again, are you?' The words were out before she had time to think of the implications. If she'd been clever she would have never let him know she'd guessed his motives.

'There is nothing to go soft about. I need to know exactly what you submitted to *World in Photographs* about my family and then we can discuss what happens next.' He opened the door of the carriage and, with a flourish of manners she knew he was displaying for the purpose of getting what he wanted, waited for her to climb in.

Emma looked from his eyes to the park around her and beyond that to the tall buildings of New York, a place she'd never been to before. What choice did she have? She was alone in a city she didn't know and pregnant with this man's baby.

'I have my laptop at the hotel, I can show you exactly what will be in it.' The painful knowledge that he'd rather discuss an article she'd written than talk about their baby cut into her. She sat in the seat, wishing she hadn't got in the carriage. The idea of playing the tourist with him again brought back heated memories of that first kiss in the sleigh.

'Did you use anything to do with what we talked about after our night together?' His voice was deep and firm, quashing those memories instantly as he snapped out the question.

'No,' she said and looked directly at him, into the depths of eyes that were shuttered, keeping her out and his thoughts locked away. 'I never wanted to pry into your family history, more to show an insight into your country. It was what Richard had suggested in the first place.'

'Who is Richard?'

'A photographer I met while on my course. He works for *World in Photographs* and helped me get the contract to write the article about your family.' She had nothing to hide, so why shouldn't she tell him about how she'd got the contract in the first place? If he chose to see it in the wrong light, that was his problem.

'What do you owe this Richard for getting you the contract?' The sharpness of his voice made her look at him quickly, but the coldness of his eyes was almost as bitter as the wind in Vladimir had been.

'Nothing. All I wanted was to take the best photographs I could and showcase your country, weaving in some of your family stories, which I have achieved without adding in anything you told me in your hotel room.'

'Then for now I trust you,' he said as the carriage

pulled away, the sudden movement making her grab the seat to steady herself. Instantly his hands reached out to hold her and from the seat opposite she felt that heated attraction connect them once more. Their eyes met; she looked into the inky blackness and swallowed as she saw the glint of steely hardness had given way to something more dangerous—desire. She couldn't allow herself to fall for his seductive charms again; she just needed to deal with the consequences of their night together and leave before she fell even further and deeper for him. Irritated by the direction of her thoughts, she pulled away and sat back in the carriage seat, desperate to avoid his scrutiny.

If he didn't trust her with his secrets then why had he told them to her? Had that also been a way of manipulating her to do what he wanted, make her think what he wanted her to think? It had not occurred to her until now that what he'd said might not have been the complete truth.

'I wouldn't lie to you, Nikolai,' she said defensively, and looked away from the dark eyes, feigning an interest in the tall buildings clearly visible above the newly green trees of the park. Maybe if she took a few shots from the carriage he'd see she was as unaffected by him as he appeared to be by her.

The lens of the camera clicked but she had no idea what she'd taken. Concentration was impossible with his dominating presence opposite her and the looming discussion of their baby. She turned the camera off and looked at him to see he'd been watching every move she'd made.

'We need to talk about our predicament.' Still his

dark eyes watched her, assessing her reaction to his words.

'Predicament?' she snapped, giving him her full attention. 'Is that what this baby is to you? A predicament? Something else you have to deal with? Just what do you suggest, Nikolai?'

'It is a predicament,' he said calmly, far too calmly, and it unnerved her. What was coming next? 'One I never wanted but one which now means we must get married.'

'Married?' she said loudly, then looked around to see if anyone had heard her. From the satisfied expression on Nikolai's face, that was exactly the reaction he had been hoping for. 'We can't get married.'

'Give me one good reason why not.' He sat back and regarded her sternly.

'We live on different continents to start with.' She grasped at the first thing she could think of and, from the amused look which crossed his face, he knew it. Why did he have to look so handsome, so incredibly sexy? And why was she still so attracted to him?

'That can easily be sorted. I have a home in London if New York isn't to your liking.' His instant response unsettled her. Had he worked it all out already?

'It's not easy for me,' she said quickly, angry that everything seemed so cut and dried with him. 'I have my sister to consider and my job. I've only just been offered a job with *World in Photographs*.'

'Your sister is in Perm for the next few years and your job could be done from anywhere, could it not?' The tone of his voice confirmed her suspicion of moments ago. He did have it all worked out—completely to suit him.

None of what he was suggesting suited her. She needed to be in London, especially now she had a job with *World in Photographs*, a job she needed for financial security, now more than ever. Not only did she have Jess to help through the ballet school, she had a baby on the way, but deep down it was more than that. His so-called deal tapped into her deepest insecurities after growing up knowing that out there in the world was her father, a man who didn't want to know her.

Overwhelmed by the panic of her situation, she glared at Nikolai. 'I need to be in London if I'm to keep the job as a photographer with *World in Photographs* and I need that job to support Jess.'

'That is easily sorted.'

She frowned, not sure what he was getting at. 'For you, maybe.'

'Jess will have all the financial help she needs to ensure she can—what was it you said in Vladimir?—chase her dream.' The look on his handsome face was as severe as she'd ever seen it, not a hint of pleasure from the generous gift he'd just offered. Or was it a gift? Was it not dangling temptation in front of her?

No, it was more than that. It was a bribe and all she had to do was marry him. The thought filled her with dread. She'd dreamed of the day a man would propose to her, dreamed of it being a loving and romantic moment. Nikolai was being neither as he sat watching her; even the ride in the carriage couldn't lend a romantic mood to the moment.

'I can't accept that,' she said, still unable to believe what was happening. He was making a deal with her for their child: marry him and she, the baby and Jess would be financially secure. It hurt that she had very little chance of ever matching that, especially now her pregnancy would affect her ability to work. If she turned him down, said no, as instinct was urging her to do, she would be turning down so much more than just a marriage proposal. She would be saying no to something which would help Jess but, more importantly, give her baby what she'd never had: a father.

Turmoil raged inside her as he watched her, the motion of the carriage making her feel slightly ill, and the steady rhythm of the horses' hooves sounding like drums in her head. How could this be happening? How could all this come from one desire-laden moment in time? How could those few blissful hours have such an impact on her life?

'No,' she said again, more firmly. 'I can't accept that.'

For a moment he looked at her and the tension between them intensified, but she refused to look away. She wanted to challenge him, wanted to push him in the same way he was pushing her.

Finally he spoke. 'Just as I will not tolerate being pushed out of my child's life, and the only way to ensure that is marriage.'

He leant forward in the carriage and she looked away, not daring to look into his dark eyes a moment longer. He had touched a raw and open wound. She was here because she'd hoped he'd want something to do with his child, that he wouldn't turn his back on either her or his baby. She'd never expected this from a man who'd declared one night was all he could give. If she turned him down, didn't that make her worse than her mother?

She couldn't help herself and looked deep into his

eyes, seeing what she'd seen that night in Vladimir, and tried to plead with him again. 'But marriage—'

'Is the only option.' He cut across her once more. 'We will be married, Emma. I will not take no for an answer, not now you are carrying my child.'

CHAPTER SIX

THE REST OF the carriage ride had blurred into a shocked haze and now, as she stood in one of New York's most renowned jeweller's, that haze was beginning to lift. She couldn't marry Nikolai. What was she thinking, allowing him to bring her here to buy an engagement ring? It wouldn't change the fact that this wasn't what he wanted. Turmoil erupted inside her. She didn't want to make the same mistakes as her mother, not when she knew what it felt like to be the child whose existence a father denied.

Could she really do this—sacrifice everything to do the right thing by her son or daughter? If she walked away now would her child blame her later, as she blamed her mother for depriving her of a father?

She looked anxiously at the door but had to steel herself against the reaction Nikolai provoked in her as he stood right behind her, so very close she could feel the heat of his body. It reminded her of the night they'd shared in Vladimir. The passion had been so intense, so powerful. Didn't the undeniable attraction count for something?

'Not thinking of running out on me, are you?' The whispered question sent a tremor of awareness down her spine, which deepened as he held the tops of her arms, pulling her back against the latent power of his body.

She shook her head in denial, unable to put a sentence together as his touch scorched through her, reminding her of the passion they'd shared the night their child had been conceived. That thought chilled the fire he'd unwittingly stirred to life just by being near her. She had to remember the cruel way he'd bargained not only with Jess's future, but her past, exploiting the one thing which had been a constant shadow in her life. Because of that, whatever she did, she had to control the desire he evoked within her from just a touch.

'No, you have made it perfectly clear what has to be done.' She turned to face him, wishing she didn't feel the rush of desire which flooded her as she looked into his eyes. They were dark and heavy with passion, just as they had been that night in Vladimir. Would she ever stop seeing images in her mind of him like that? He'd become imprinted there and he invaded every thought. Had it been because he was the only man to have touched her intimately, the only man she'd made love with or simply the worry of facing him to tell him about the baby?

A heaviness settled over her as an ominous clarity finally allowed her to see that night for what it really was. It had just been a seduction, a way to keep her from whatever it was he was hiding, and for him it most definitely hadn't been about making love. For him it would have been purely lust.

'Then I suggest we select the ring that will seal the deal.' His voice sounded firm and in control. Yet again he was manipulating her, forcing her to accept his terms.

Panic filled Emma. This wasn't how she'd envisaged the moment she would get engaged. It had been very much more romantic than this demand that she choose a ring. But what choice did she have now? Not only would he provide the funds for Jess, he would be in his child's life. It was exactly how she'd always envisaged being a mother—supported by the child's father. The only difference was that in her dreams that man had been there for her too—out of love, not duty to his child.

'You're right,' she said calmly, reluctantly acknowledging this was the only way forward.

Further doubts crowded in on her, solidifying the need to accept Nikolai's deal, no matter what she felt. What if she couldn't cope, just as her mother hadn't been able to do? Would her baby be taken from her, as she and Jess had been? That wouldn't happen if she was married to the child's father.

'So, are we agreed?' he asked in a calm voice.

'Yes,' she replied, seeing no other option but this deal he'd given her. 'This is the best way.'

Before she could back out of the marriage she'd agreed to, with a man she'd never expected to see again after he'd left her at the hotel, she gave her full attention to the rings displayed before her. The sparkling stones blurred for a moment and she blinked to try and refocus them, horrified to realise it was tears filling her eyes that were distorting the almost endless display of expensive rings.

Once she'd selected one of the rings and was wearing it the deal would be sealed. She would have accepted his terms. She blinked quickly once more, trying to stop the threatening tears from falling. She couldn't cry. Not yet. She had to be as strong and detached as he was being.

'I think an emerald.' He moved to her side and put his arm around her, his hand holding her waist as he pulled her tighter against his body. 'To match your eyes.'

He'd noticed she had green eyes? That snippet of information shocked her, because it meant he had taken an interest in her beyond the seduction he'd obviously been planning since the ride in the troika. The memory of that day was now tarnished by the reality of the fact that he'd engineered it all—and she'd fallen for it. Had that wonderfully gentle yet powerfully seductive kiss been part of the plan too?

Of course it had and you fell for it.

'How about this one?' she asked, tiredness washing over her, brought on no doubt by the stress of everything, combined with the time difference and pregnancy. All she wanted to do right now was get back to her hotel room and rest, but she held the ring up by the delicate diamond-encrusted band, the emerald sparkling in the bright lights of the store.

'Are you sure you wouldn't prefer one of the larger ones?' He moved away from her and sat in a distinctly antique-looking chair to the side of the table. She tried hard not to look at his long legs as he stretched them out before him. He looked far too relaxed when she was as tense as she'd ever been.

'No,' she said and looked boldly into his eyes, not missing the way his gaze slid down her body before meeting hers. The tingle of awareness was disconcerting and she pushed it aside, determined to be in control of this moment at the very least. 'No, this is much more my style.'

He stood up and came back to her. He took the ring from her, looking at it, then, to her astonishment, took her left hand in his, raising it up. With deliberate slowness he slipped the ring onto her finger and she was amazed to see it was a perfect fit, as if it had been made for her. 'In that case, will you do me the honour of becoming my wife?'

It was the last thing she'd expected him to do after having all but put a deal to her and she stumbled over her words, aware of the store staff watching the exchange. Was this all for their benefit or his? She looked at him, wondering if she'd be able to speak, but finally the words came out in a soft whisper. 'Yes, Nikolai, I will.'

He kept hold of her hand for far too long and she watched as he looked down at the square emerald now sat neatly on her finger. Would he keep his side of this strange bargain? Would he provide the funds for Jess to continue on her chosen course in life and, more importantly, be there for his child?

If he doesn't you only have to walk away; you have nothing to lose by agreeing.

As that rebellious thought rocked through her he stepped closer and lowered his head; she knew, with every nerve in her body, that he was going to kiss her. Right there in the store.

When his lips met hers fire shot through her and her knees weakened and, as her eyes fluttered closed, she forced them open again. He moved slightly and she could see his lips lifting into a smile that was full of self-satisfaction. Then he spoke so softly only she could hear. 'A very sensible answer.'

Nikolai opened the door of the car he'd ordered while he'd completed his purchase for the engagement ring—an item he'd never envisaged buying again. But what choice did he have? He couldn't turn his back on his child. This was his chance to prove to himself he was a better man than his father. His child had not been conceived in the underhand way he himself had been, so didn't that already make him a better man? But it wasn't enough. He needed to prove to himself he was not like his father.

He watched as Emma slid into the back of the car, looking weary, and a pang of guilt briefly touched him. He had nothing to feel guilty about, he reassured himself. Emma was here to secure her and her child's future and, now that he'd also added her sister's into the bargain, she had everything she'd come for—and more.

She would become his fiancée and, as soon as possible, his wife. He wanted this particular deal sealed long before news of their baby broke. He wanted his mother to think he'd found love and happiness. It was all she'd ever wanted for him and now, due to one night when he'd been less than in control, he was able to give her that.

'Where are you staying?' he demanded as he joined her in the back of the car.

'A hotel on West Forty-Seventh Street,' she said without looking at him, provoking that twinge of guilt once more as he gave the driver instructions.

'This is the right thing to do,' he said as he took her hand from where it lay in her lap. She turned to look at him, her sable hair moving invitingly, reminding him of how soft it had been between his fingers.

'What if you meet someone you really want to marry?' The doubt laced in her voice did little to soften the emotions running through him. As far as he was concerned, that would never be an issue. The example of married life his father had set him was one which had stayed with him long after his mother had found happiness. He might have seen her marry for love when he was almost twelve years old but inside he knew he had his father's genes. The way to avoid testing that theory had been to avoid any kind of emotional commitment. By the time he'd become a successful businessman in his own right, he'd also become cold and cynical and knew he would never think of marrying— at least, not for love.

'That won't be an issue. I could, of course, ask the same of you.'

'Oh, I always dreamed of the fairy-tale wedding. You know—big white dress, flower girls and bridesmaids, fancy location and a honeymoon in a tropical paradise.' At first he was taken aback by her soft, wistful voice, but the hard glint in those green eyes warned him it was just a cover-up. He knew all about hiding emotions, only he was better at it than she was; but he'd play the game her way. For now, at least.

'And now?'

'Now?' She pulled her hand free of his and glared up at him, defiance adding to the sparks in her eyes. 'Now I know better.'

'So you won't be looking for love and happy-ever-afters?'

'Never.' That one word was said with so much conviction he didn't doubt it for one minute.

'Then we agree on that too. You see, already we have a good base for our marriage. A child who needs us both and an obvious dislike of anything remotely romantic.'

She looked at him, questions racing across her beautiful face, and all he wanted to do was taste her lips once more. The memory of that kiss in the snow had lingered in his mind for the best part of two months, just as the hours spent making her truly his had filled his dreams night after night. It had been those memories which had made kissing her in the store impossible to resist, that and the smouldering anger, defused by an undeniable attraction in her alluring eyes.

'We're here,' she said quickly, the relief in her voice more than evident.

'I'll come with you whilst you check out,' he said as he got out of the car into the bustle of New York's streets.

'I'm not checking out,' she said sternly as she joined him, defiantly glaring up at him.

'We are now engaged—you will not stay here alone; besides, we have a party to plan.' Did she really expect him to leave her here after the news she'd given him today? He wasn't going to give her any opportunity to run out on him again, which he suspected was exactly what she wanted to do.

'What party?' The shock in her voice angered him more than he was comfortable with. It seemed everything today was out of his comfort zone.

'Our engagement party. I'll call the planner as soon as we get back to my apartment. I think the weekend

would be best.' Before she could say anything, he took
her arm and propelled her into the sleek interior of the
hotel. 'But first you need to collect your luggage and
check out.'

Emma couldn't believe how things were going. She'd
had no idea what to expect when she'd made the journey to New York, but it wasn't this. She walked across
the spacious apartment which gave stunning views
over Central Park and that feeling of disbelief that he'd
insisted she check out of the hotel intensified. 'There
was no need for me to leave the hotel.'

'There is every need, Emma. Apart from the engagement party, which is scheduled for the weekend,
I want you to rest.' The authority in his voice was unmistakable. She wanted to rebel against it but, just as
she had done when she and Jess had moved from one
foster family to another, she held it back. It was a skill
she'd become adept at over the years.

Nikolai strode across the polished wooden floor to
stand looking out of the large floor-to-ceiling windows and seeing his solitary figure reminded her of the
photo she'd taken at his family home. He'd looked desolate and alone then. Now the firm set of his shoulders
warned her he was far from desolate and very much in
control of the situation and his emotions.

She wished she had her camera in her hands right
now but instead walked softly across the floor to join
him, her footsteps light. Just remembering him like that
had calmed her emotions, made her want to find again
the companionship they had experienced in Vladimir
before they'd spent the night together. Maybe, if they

could find that, then this marriage she was about to make had a chance of success.

She was fully aware the attraction was still there, the chemistry that sparked to life from just a single touch. His kiss as they were buying the ring had proved that, but if they were to make this work they needed to be friends; they needed to be able to hold a simple conversation without being on guard.

'That's quite a view,' she said as she stood next to him, hoping to make light conversation about something neutral. He didn't look at her and she glanced at his strong profile. 'I'd like to take some photographs, perhaps as the sun sets.'

'So that you can sell them?' Harshness had crept back into his voice and he turned to face her. 'Is that what this is all about? Extracting yet more from me and my family? Exposing even more details to bargain for money?'

As his words sank in she realised with shock what he was asking. 'It's not about that at all, Nikolai, I just wanted to take the photographs for my own enjoyment. I've never been to New York, let alone in a swanky apartment with views over Central Park.'

'I haven't yet seen what you submitted to *World in Photographs*.' He turned to look at her, his dark eyes black with veiled anger.

'That is easily sorted,' she said as she headed to the room he'd had her small amount of luggage delivered to. She'd been relieved to discover that he had no intention of spending the night in the same bed as her, but to her dismay that relief had been tinged with disappointment.

When she returned to the large open-plan living

space of the apartment, he was still looking out of the window, his shoulders more tense than ever. What was he so worried about? What could a few photographs and a small piece about his family really do?

She put her laptop down on the table and fired it up, the question as to what he was so worried about going round in her mind. All families had troubles they kept hidden from the world. She knew that more than most. She opened the piece she'd written for *World in Photographs* to go with the stunning images she'd taken and stepped away from the table.

'It's there for you. Richard liked it,' she said softly and sat down on the large cream sofa which dominated one corner of the apartment.

'Richard has seen it?' From across the room, Nikolai glared at her.

'He's been very helpful, and I wouldn't have got that contract without his help.' She fixed her gaze on the view of the park, not daring to look at him as he walked towards her laptop and began reading.

After five minutes of heavy silence he turned to look at her, his handsome face set in a forbidding frown. 'This is what you submitted?'

'Yes; what did you expect, Nikolai?'

'Not this light-hearted, romantic stuff about life in Russia. You have turned what I told you into something quite different.'

He walked towards her, his footsteps hard on the polished wooden floor, and she wished she hadn't chosen to sit down. He was too imposing, too dominating. 'You told me very little, Nikolai, and as I didn't get to meet with your grandmother I had to come up with something.'

'None of it true.'

'What is the truth, Nikolai? Why were you so worried I would meet your grandmother?'

He sighed and sat down next to her on the sofa, the air around them suddenly charged with something she couldn't yet fathom out. 'My family's story is complicated.'

'I know all about complicated, Nikolai. Jess and I have experienced it first-hand.' Why had she said that? She wanted to find out about him, not spill out her own sorry story. Would he still want her as his wife if he knew what kind of upbringing she'd had?

'Then we have that in common at least.' Sadness tinged his voice and her heart constricted, just as it had done when she'd taken the photo of him outside the ruins of what had once been his family home. She wanted to reach out to him, but kept her hands firmly together in her lap.

'Do you want to talk about it?' she asked, knowing full well he didn't, that he wanted to keep it all hidden safely away. It was what she'd done all through her childhood, mostly to protect Jess, who didn't know half of it.

'No but, as you are soon to marry into my family, then you should know.'

Her mouth went dry with fear. Would that mean he too would want to know about her childhood, her family? 'You don't have to tell me anything you don't want to.'

'You should know something of how I came to be living in New York and why I no longer use Petrushov, the surname I was born with.'

She looked at him, unable to stop herself from

reaching out to touch him. She placed her hand on his arm, trying to ignore the jolt of something wild which sparked between them from that innocent touch. 'We don't have to do this now.'

He ignored her and continued, his face a firm mask of composure. 'My mother's marriage to my father was not happy, neither was my childhood, and when he died it was a release for both my mother and I.'

'I'm sorry,' she said softly but her words didn't seem to reach him. Instead they only brought forward her own painful childhood memories—and she wasn't ready to share them yet.

'My mother was helped by a business acquaintance of my father and I guess it was one of those rare moments when love conquered all.' He looked down at her hand, still on his arm, and frowned, as if he'd only just realised she was touching him. Obviously her touch didn't do to him what his did to her.

'You say that as if you don't believe in such a concept.' She pulled her hand back and kept it firmly in her lap.

'I thought we'd already established that love is something neither of us believe in.' His dark eyes bored into hers, accusation and suspicion filling them, and she recalled their conversation in Vladimir. She remembered being blasé about looking for a fairy-tale wedding and happy-ever-after. She knew no such thing would ever happen to her, but from the way he was looking at her now he thought she wanted such things.

'We did; you just threw me when you said it was one of "those rare moments". As if you really believe they happen.' She smiled at him, injecting lightness into her voice. It was far better he thought she didn't believe in love in any shape or form. The last thing he needed to know right now was that she did believe in love and happy-ever-afters; she just didn't believe it would ever happen to her. It never would now she'd agreed to marry him as part of a deal.

'Well, whatever you believe, it happened for my mother. She changed from the constantly scared woman who lingered in the shadows of her marriage and blossomed into someone very different—and it's all thanks to Roger Cunningham. Even in my early teens I could see that, and at sixteen I changed my surname legally to his, although I'd already spent all my years here in New York as Nikolai Cunningham.'

'I did wonder,' she said, remembering his insistence that his name wasn't Petrushov when she'd first met him, and the card he'd tossed on the bed just before walking out on her. She pushed the pain of that moment aside and focused on the present. 'And now your child will take that name too.'

'As will you when we are married.' He looked at her hand, at the emerald ring on her finger, and she wondered if he was regretting what had seemed an impulsive move, telling her they would be married.

'We don't have to get married, Nikolai. I would never keep you from your child, not after having grown up without a father myself.' She swallowed down the nerves as she waited for his response. He looked into her eyes, as if he was trying to read her thoughts, and as much as she wanted to look away she held his gaze.

'Is the idea of being my wife that abhorrent to you?' His voice had deepened and a hint of an accent she'd never noticed before came through. The idea of being married was terrifying, but the idea of being this man's wife was less so. Was that because he was the only man she had truly known?

She shook her head, not able to speak.

He lifted his hand and pushed her hair back from her face. 'I will never do anything to hurt you, Emma; you do know that, don't you?'

The words were so tender she had to swallow down the urge to cry. His fingers brushed her cheek, bringing their night together vividly back to her mind. 'Yes, I know that.'

He leant towards her, his hand sliding round beneath her hair, holding her head gently, and before she could say or do anything his lips were on hers, the same gentle, teasing kiss as in the store. Her resistance melted like ice-cream on a hot day and she kissed him back. He deepened the kiss, sending a fury of fireworks around her body, reviving all the desire she'd felt for him and, if the truth were told, still felt even though she'd supressed it well.

She still wanted him, still yearned for him.

'We still have the passion we found in Vladimir,' he said as he broke the kiss and moved away from her, leaving her almost shuddering from the heat coursing through her. 'And that at least will make our marriage more bearable.'

She blinked in shock at his words. He'd been toying with her, proving his point. He obviously would never have chosen her to be his wife if it wasn't for the baby, but he'd told her he'd never wanted to be married when he'd first met her. She'd already accepted it was what she had to do for Jess as much as the baby. 'It will, yes.'

He smiled at her, but the warmth didn't reach those black eyes. 'Then we shall marry in three weeks. But first, there is the small matter of an engagement party.'

CHAPTER SEVEN

THE WEEK HAD flown by in a whirl of party arrangements and now it was time to face not only Nikolai's friends as his fiancée but his mother and stepfather. Emma's nerves jangled as she waited and she thought back to those two kisses on the day they'd become engaged. She had thought they were a positive sign, that he did at least feel something for her, but for the last week he'd withdrawn into his work and she had spent much of the time out with her camera.

Just this morning she'd been shopping in a store Nikolai had instructed her to visit for a dress suitable for the glamorous event the engagement party had turned into; now she stood looking out over a city which never slept, wearing the kind of dress she'd never imagined possible and feeling more like Cinderella every minute. The only thing she needed was Prince Charming to declare his undying love and sweep her away for a happy-ever-after but she doubted Nikolai would be willing to play that role.

She'd been in the beauty salon for the early part of the afternoon, nerves building with each passing hour. The cream dress, encrusted with beads, fitted to perfection and when she'd looked in the mirror before leaving her room she hadn't recognised herself. The woman Nikolai had met in Vladimir had gone, replaced by someone who looked much more polished and refined. What would Nikolai think of that? Or had it been his intention all along to mould her into the woman he wanted her to be?

She heard Nikolai's footsteps and nerves filled her so quickly she didn't want to turn round, but knew she would have to. When she did her breath caught in her throat. She'd seen him in a suit, but never a tuxedo, and the image he created stirred more than just her creative mind.

The fine black cloth hugged his broad shoulders, caressed his biceps and followed his lean frame downwards. The crisp white shirt set off the black tie to perfection, but it was his face which drew her attention far more. Stubble which had been tamed to look effortlessly sexy covered his jawline, emphasising the firm set of his lips. Dark hair was styled into conformity but a few locks were already breaking free and forming curls at his temples.

'You look…' he said softly as he stood and fastened his cufflinks, the movement showing off his wrists and designer watch. His dark eyes were full of controlled anger as he sought the words he was looking for.

'Very different.' She didn't want to hear what he thought and finished the sentence for him. All she wanted was to get his charade over with. She hated the pretence of it all.

He stepped a little closer, dropping his arms by his side, making the cloth of the tuxedo cling even more provocatively to him. 'I was going to say very beautiful.'

'I'm not so sure about that.' She blushed beneath his scrutiny and clutched her bag ever tighter.

She was about to walk past him when he caught her arm, the look in his eyes heavy with desire; as much as she wanted to look away, to avoid the way her body sizzled with pleasure, she boldly met his gaze. She stood there, locked in time, waiting for him to say something. He didn't and finally he let go of her, the connection gone, snuffed out like a candle, leaving a lingering scent in the air.

'We should go. My mother will be expecting us.' He turned away from her, as if he'd made a mistake even touching her, and she wasn't sure what worried her the most: the thought of meeting his mother and stepfather or that he couldn't bear to look at her.

'I'm looking forward to meeting her,' she said as she fiddled with her bag, anything other than witness his obvious discomfort at being around her.

'There is one thing I need to ask from you.' He stopped at the door of the apartment and looked down at her. 'My mother knows nothing of the baby and I'd like to keep it that way. For now, at least.'

He was ashamed of her, ashamed of the child she carried. That hurt her more than anything, but it also showcased the fact that this marriage was nothing more than a deal and she must never fall into the trap of thinking it was anything else.

She frowned and tried to smile, but she couldn't help but ask, 'Why?'

'She believes I am in love. We are in love. I want to keep it that way. I want her to believe we are marrying simply because we fell in love.' Each time he said the word 'love', his voice became harsher, as if he couldn't bear even naming such an emotion.

So he was ashamed he was to be a father. Was that why he wanted to get married as soon as possible—so that he could make it look like something they'd planned or at least wanted?

She shrugged, trying to hide her hurt at what he'd just said. 'If that's what you want.'

Nikolai watched as his mother hugged Emma, then held her hands and stood back to look at her, as if shocked that he'd finally brought a woman home to meet her. His gaze lingered a little too long on Emma's glorious body, encased in a gown which caressed her figure in a way that evoked memories of kissing her all over before making her his—truly his.

'I am so pleased to meet you.' His mother's words dragged his mind back from the erotic path they had taken, forcing him to concentrate on the present. 'I never really believed I'd see this day; and such a gorgeous ring.'

'A gorgeous ring for a very beautiful woman.' Nikolai spoke his thoughts aloud before he had time to evaluate them, but when Emma blushed and his mother smiled he knew they had been exactly what was needed.

'You must of course stay here tonight,' his mother offered Emma, just as she had done with him earlier in the week, but he'd refused, claiming a need to work the next day.

'Emma and I will be travelling back tonight,' he said sternly and felt Emma's gaze on him. Was she pleading with him to extricate them both from the invitation?

'I won't hear of it. How can you enjoy your engagement party if you have to travel back tonight? Besides, I've already had a room prepared, so there is no excuse.'

'I need to be at the office first thing in the morning.' Nikolai knew his voice sounded abrupt and, if the curious glance Emma cast his way was anything to go by, his mother would know he was making excuses.

'Nonsense. You work far too hard, and besides, it's the weekend and you should be spending it with your fiancée. Isn't that right, Emma?' His mother smiled at him, using her charm and tactics as she always did to get what she wanted, but he didn't want Emma pushed into a situation that she clearly didn't want. Also, staying here at his mother's house in The Hamptons would almost certainly mean sharing not only a room with Emma, but a bed. The fact that his mother had made a room ready suggested she'd already planned it all out.

'I don't have anything with me, Mrs Cunningham.' Emma's soft voice caught him unawares, as did the way it sent a tingle of awareness down his spine. He looked at her, at the worried expression on her face, and something twisted inside him, as if his heart was being squeezed.

He couldn't be falling for her. He didn't want that kind of complication, especially when she was here to celebrate their engagement only because he'd made a deal which would secure not only her baby's future but her sister's. A deal she'd been more than happy to agree on once he'd made her see that refusal would leave her child without a father. Something he knew she was all too familiar with.

'Well, if that's the only reason, I can soon sort that

out. My stepdaughter is here with her husband and between us both we can loan you anything you need.'

Nikolai's control on the situation was slipping through his fingers and he was torn between saving Emma from being forced to spend a night in the same room as him and allowing his mother to continue with the illusion that he'd finally succumbed to love.

'I couldn't do that…' Emma began, but before she could finish he spoke over her.

'Then we shall stay.' He pulled Emma against him, the fine fabric of her dress no barrier to the heat from her body as it seared through his suit, setting him alight with a desire he had no intention of acting on. Diversion was what he needed. 'We should mingle.'

At the extravagantly laid tables all around them were friends and members of his family, or rather his stepfamily. Everyone was enjoying themselves and their laughter mixed with the music from the live performers. He and Emma were the centre of attention, and that was something he hadn't thought of when he'd put the party planners in touch with his mother and let them loose together. A big mistake.

'I'm sorry,' he said as he took Emma's hand and led her to a table where they could sit and try and keep out of the limelight, for a while at least.

'For what?' She sat elegantly beside him and again that strange sensation washed over him.

'There isn't anyone here you know.'

'That's okay,' she answered as she looked around the marquee, hardly recognisable beneath its lavish decorations. 'It's not as if it's a real engagement.'

'It's very real, Emma.' Anger surfaced, smothering the simmering desire which brewed deep inside him.

She turned in her seat to give him her full attention and all he could do was look at her lips, red with lipstick, and imagine kissing them until she sighed with pleasure. He couldn't let her do this to him. He had to get back his control and fast. 'We are engaged and will be married by the end of the month.'

'But it's not for real, Nikolai, despite what you want your mother to believe. None of it is real—and I can't do this again.' A look of fear flitted across her face and he frowned in confusion.

'Do what?' He took her hands from her lap, where she'd clutched them tightly together. She looked at him, directly into his eyes, and he saw the anguish in hers.

'Be paraded around like this. When we get married, I want it to be with as little fuss as possible. I don't want to be the subject of everyone's scrutiny.' Her green eyes pleaded with him and the slight waver in her voice unsettled him. Was she having second thoughts about their deal?

'That suits me perfectly.' He snapped the words out and let her hands go, angered by the thought that she was at this very moment looking for a way out of their planned marriage—and the deal.

Emma didn't want the party to end. It was so lavish she could hardly have dreamed it up if she'd tried, and if she and Nikolai had truly been in love it would have been the perfect start to their life together. But they weren't in love. Nikolai's stern words as they'd sat talking at the beginning of the evening had been more than enough proof for her.

'Emma, Nikolai.' His mother came up to them, excitement all over her face. 'It's time for the finale, and

I want you to be in the prime spot when it happens. Come with me.'

'What have you done now?' Nikolai's deep voice demanded of his mother, but she wasn't listening, and she headed off through the crowds, leaving them no choice but to follow her out and across the lawns. Emma could hear the water in the darkness which surrounded the extensive garden, now lit up with hundreds of lights, and it was a relief to be away from the many people who had attended the party, none of whom she knew.

'I have no idea what this is about,' Nikolai said sternly, his irritation at such a public display of them as a newly engaged couple all too obvious.

'We should at least see,' she said to Nikolai, unable to supress a smile. How nice it must be to have a mother who would arrange surprises for you; it was exactly the kind of mother she wanted to be herself.

Nikolai didn't say anything, but took her hand and made his way to where his mother was talking to a group of people. His annoyance at the arrangement was very clear.

'Stand here, with the party as a backdrop. I want an engagement photo of you both.' The excitement in his mother's voice was contagious and Emma couldn't help but laugh softly. Nikolai didn't share her appreciation and wasn't in the least amused by it.

'That's not necessary.' Nikolai's brusque tone didn't make a dent on his mother's enthusiasm.

At that point Emma realised this wasn't just a snapshot for a family album, as a party photographer joined them and set about making them stand just where he wanted them to. Instantly she was uncomfortable. She hated being on what she considered the wrong side of the lens.

'Now, embrace each other,' the photographer said as he stepped back and started clicking, his assistants altering lights to get the best result. 'Kiss each other.' Kiss.

Emma looked at Nikolai and wondered just what he was going to say about being forced to kiss her. The same kind of boldness which had come over her in Vladimir rushed through her again.

'We'd better do as we're told,' she whispered with a smile on her lips, amused at his hard expression. He wasn't doing a very good job of acting the part of a man in love, which was what he'd wanted his mother to think he was. 'We're in love, remember?'

His eyes darkened until they were so black and full of desire that she caught her breath as anticipation rushed through her. Her heart thumped harder and she was sure he'd see the pulse at her throat, but his gaze didn't waver. He pulled her closer against him and she could feel his thighs touch hers, his chest press against her breasts.

He moved slowly but with intent purpose until his lips met hers and, acting on instinct, her eyes closed and her body melted into his. His arms held her tighter still and she wrapped hers around his neck as he deepened the kiss. She didn't want to respond, didn't want to acknowledge the power of the passion racing through her, but she couldn't help herself. She opened her lips and tasted his with her tongue as fireworks seemed to explode around them.

'Perfect,' the photographer directed. 'Keep kissing her.'

Nikolai's hand slid down to the small of her back, pressing her against him, and the fire of desire raged through her. If she didn't stop him now she'd be in danger of giving herself away, of allowing him to see just what he did to her.

She let her arms fall from his neck and pushed against his chest, wanting to continue, yet not wanting him to know that just a kiss could make her his again. 'That's pretty powerful acting,' she said, alarmed at how husky her voice sounded.

A large bang sounded behind them and, startled, she looked towards the party. Fireworks filled the night sky behind the marquee and relief washed over her. She thought she had heard fireworks as he'd kissed her, ones created by this man's kiss. The relief at discovering that they had been real made her laugh and, still in Nikolai's embrace, she looked up at him.

'The same can be said of you.' Desire filled his voice as he responded.

Nikolai let her go as his mother walked towards them, a big smile on her face. 'That was perfect. I will see you both in the morning.'

Emma watched her leave, an ultra-glamorous woman who believed her son had found the love of his life. What would she say if she knew the truth, and why was it so important to Nikolai that she thought that? Questions burned in her mind.

'Shall we return to the party or retire to bed?' The question shocked her and she didn't know which was more preferable. She didn't want to continue to be the centre of speculation but neither did she want to go to their room.

'Perhaps we should just go back to your apartment.'

The suggestion came from her before she had time to think.

'I can see that my presence in your room is not going to be welcome, but I can assure you, nothing will happen. The pretence of being in love can be dropped once we close the bedroom door.'

'In that case, we should retire,' she said, trying to keep the despondency from her voice. He didn't want her, didn't find her attractive. The kiss of moments ago had been just an act. Pretence at attraction and love, purely to keep his mother happy.

Nikolai saw the expression of horror cross Emma's face, and wished he'd been firmer with his mother, but she'd looked so happy he just couldn't destroy that for her. This whole sham of an engagement was to make his mother happy and now he was guilty of making Emma unhappy. Strangely, that was worse, but it was too late to back out now. They would spend the night in this room and leave as soon as they could in the morning.

Emma crossed the room to the only bed and looked at the items his mother had instructed to be left for them. She held up a cream silk nightdress which would do little to conceal her figure and he closed his eyes against the image of her in it—and, worse, next to him in that very bed.

'It appears your mother has thought of everything,' she said as she looked up at him. 'It's almost as if she was planning on us having to stay.'

Emma had just echoed his own thoughts, but he brushed them away in an attempt to put her at ease. 'Whatever it was my mother had planned, she believes we are in love and, as I said earlier, I want to keep it that way. I also promised that nothing would happen between us, so I will sleep in the chair.'

He gestured to an easy chair which would be perfect for relaxing in during the day, but not so great to sleep in for a night. She looked from him to the chair and sighed, as if in resignation.

'I hardly think that will be conducive to a good night's sleep.' He was about to argue the point when a smile tugged at the corners of her mouth. 'We'll just have to manage together in the bed. We are, after all, both adults and have agreed that nothing is going to happen.'

He might have agreed, but he seriously doubted if he could carry through that promise. She stood before him now in the dress which shimmered in the lights of the room, and he wanted her more than he'd ever wanted any woman.

Maybe one more night in her arms would be enough to suppress the desire-laden thoughts he constantly had about her? That question sent a rush of lust sparking around him, but as he looked at her worried expression he knew it couldn't happen. Not after he'd been the one to set the time limit—just one night in Vladimir.

'In that case, I suggest we get some sleep.' He pulled off his tie and tossed it onto the chair he'd planned to sleep in, determined to prove to himself he was able to exercise firm control where this woman was concerned. Emma didn't move. 'Is there a problem?'

'Can you unzip me?'

She blushed and looked more beautiful and innocent than she'd ever done, but there was a hint of humour in her voice. Did she know just how much she was torturing him?

'I had help this afternoon, but I don't have a stylist to hand at present. Thanks for arranging all that; it was very thoughtful.'

He walked towards her, wondering if he trusted himself to be so close to her, undoing the dress he'd wanted to remove from her sexy body all night. She was testing him, pushing him to the limits of his endurance, whether she knew it or not.

'I wanted you to look the part,' he said, then added more gently as her perfume weaved around him, drawing him ever closer like a ship lured to the rocks by a raging storm, 'And you looked beautiful—so very beautiful.'

'I felt beautiful,' she whispered, as if letting him hear her thoughts. 'It was a fairy-tale night.'

'My mother believes in that fairy tale, at least,' he said firmly, desperate to remind himself why he was even here like this with her. 'You played your part well.'

She looked up at him as he stood in front of her, boldly locking her gaze with his in a fleeting gesture of defiance before lowering her lashes and looking away. She turned her back to him and lifted up her hair, which hung in a glossy veil down her back, exposing the silky, smooth skin he remembered from their night together.

His hand lingered on the zip. He couldn't let go, couldn't step away from the temptation she was creating. He could see her spine and curled his fingers tight against the need to trail them up it and then all the way down. He wanted to kiss her back, to take every last piece of clothing from her sexy body and kiss her everywhere, before claiming her as his once more.

He bit down on a powerful rush of desire which surged through him. Not only had she made it clear she didn't want him, he didn't want the complications of sex becoming something more. He had to ignore the lust which was rapidly engulfing him, if only to prove to himself he didn't want her, didn't feel anything for her.

He reached out and gently pulled the zip downwards, inwardly groaning as her back became visible. The heat of passion was rushing straight to his groin. If this was any other woman, or any other moment in time, he would be kissing that wonderfully bare back and sliding the dress from her, exposing her near nakedness to his hungry gaze. But this wasn't any other woman. This was the woman who was to become his wife and everything was so very complicated.

'Thank you.' She stepped away from him and he clenched his fingers tightly to prevent himself from doing anything else.

Passion pounded in his body, begging for release as she turned to face him. Her hardened nipples were clearly visible through the fine material and he wondered how he'd never noticed until now she was braless. The thought shifted the demanding desire inside him up several notches, ever closer to breaking point.

The air hummed with heavy desire as she picked up the nightdress his mother had magically found from somewhere and walked into the adjoining bathroom and closed the door. For a moment, relief washed over him until he realised that when she returned she'd be wearing even less. The cream nightdress would offer even less protection from him.

With an angry growl he took off his jacket and slung it over the back of the chair. What the hell was wrong with him? He'd never been a slave to desire. He was always in control. *Except with this woman.*

As the bathroom door opened he crossed the room, not daring to look at her, not wanting to see her wearing the silky nightdress which would reveal far more of her body than he could tolerate. He kept his back to her as he heard the bedcovers being moved and then headed for the bathroom. Once inside, he shut the door firmly and turned on the shower, selecting the coldest setting.

When he returned to the bedroom, invigorated from the icy cold jets of water, Emma was lying in the bed, as far to one edge of it as was possible, and either asleep or pretending to be. Wearing only his underwear, he slid beneath the cool covers, turned off the light and lay on his back, looking up at the ceiling through the darkness. Anger boiled up in him, thankfully dimming the throb of desire, allowing his usual stern control to return.

Emma sighed softly next to him and turned over, moving closer to him. He lay rigid in the bed as her breathing settled into the soft rhythm of sleep again. He could feel the warmth of her body, and in his mind all he could see was her naked in his bed in Vladimir. Nothing had changed. He couldn't relax. Damn it, he'd never sleep.

He closed his eyes, willing his body to relax, and, just when he thought he might achieve that elusive state, Emma stirred and moved again. Closer to him. Far too close. She put her arm across his chest and pulled herself closer, pressing her body against the side of his, and instantly his body was ready for her. He clenched his jaw tightly, fighting the throb of desire and the urge to turn to her, to wrap her in his arms and kiss her awake before making her his once more.

A feral curse slipped from his lips as she sighed once more, pressing herself tighter against him so that he could feel the swell of her breast against his arm. He couldn't move. He didn't trust himself to. He had to prove he was stronger than the desire he had for her, something he'd never had a problem with before.

How could he want her so much? What had she done to him? Questions raced through his mind and he focused on them instead of the heady warmth of Emma's sleeping body next to his.

Never in his life had he spent a night with a woman without having sex. How had it come to this? He tried again to sleep, to ignore the heat of her body, and it was more than torture as he lay rigid next to the one woman who threatened everything, from his sanity to his family. How the hell could he want her so badly?

CHAPTER EIGHT

EMMA BLUSHED AGAIN as memories from the few hours they'd spent in bed together came rushing back to her. She still couldn't believe that she'd been wrapped around Nikolai when she'd woken. She'd opened her eyes as spring sunshine had streamed into the unfamiliar room, wondering at first where she was. Then she'd realised they were entwined, as if they were lovers. Slowly she'd moved away from Nikolai as he slept, taking the chance to steal a glance at his handsome features before slipping away to put on a dress left for her last night.

Had anything happened? Had she embarrassed herself by saying or doing something stupid in a sleepy state? She hoped she hadn't let her growing feelings for him show—especially as he'd been adamant that nothing would happen between them. So many questions had raced around her mind as they'd left the beautiful house and started the drive back to his apartment in New York. A tense silence had enveloped them in the car and she hadn't been about to break it, especially not by asking about last night.

Now they were back in his apartment and she was lying in her bed alone, replaying the events of the party.

The kiss for their engagement photo had been so powerful, so very evocative, she'd thought it was real, but then he'd pulled away from her, the hardness of his eyes warning her against such thoughts. But it was when he'd helped her out of her dress that things really had changed. She'd seen raw desire in his eyes as he'd looked at her, and when he'd touched her she'd clamped her mouth tightly closed, worried she might say something and give herself away—because she'd wanted him to touch her.

She should be grateful he hadn't said a word about the previous night other than to make small talk about the party itself, but she wasn't. It didn't feel right, ignoring whatever it was that sizzled between them. With a huff of irritation, she flung back the covers. There was no way she could sleep now. Her mind was alive with questions and her body still yearned for a man who didn't want her.

Silently she left her room and padded across the polished wooden floor to the kitchen as the sounds of a city which never seemed to sleep played out in the background. Was this what her life would be like from now on? Would she be hiding an ever-deepening affection for the father of her child for ever? Could she live like that?

She poured some water and went to sit by the windows, needing the peaceful view of the park to soothe her tortured emotions. She just couldn't be falling for Nikolai, not when all she'd wanted was that happy-ever-after with a man who loved her. But she'd never get that happiness now, even by marrying Nikolai. He didn't love her and had made it clear their marriage was to be nothing more than a deal.

'Are you unwell?' Nikolai's voice startled her, but when she looked up she was even more startled. Just as he'd done that night in Vladimir, he'd pulled on a pair of jeans, and looked so incredibly sexy she had to stop herself from taking in a deep and shuddering breath.

'I couldn't sleep.' She tried hard to avert her gaze from his bare chest, but couldn't. All she could think about was lying with her arms across it last night. She could still feel the muscles beneath her palm and distinctly remembered the scent of his aftershave invading her sleep. What else was she going to remember?

'But you are feeling quite well?' The concern in his voice was touching and she smiled at him.

'I'm fine, just not sleepy.' She didn't have much chance of feeling sleepy now after seeing him like that. All her senses were on high alert, her body all but tuned into his.

His gaze travelled down her bare legs and she realised how she must look, sat on the sofa wearing only a vest top and skimpy shorts, but there wasn't anything she could do about it now, not without alerting him to the fact that she was far from comfortable having a discussion with him when they were both half-undressed. It was much too intimate.

'Is it because you are alone tonight? Nobody to curl up with?' The seductive huskiness of his voice held a hint of laughter. Was he making fun of her?

She looked up at him and knew that wasn't true. He moved closer and stood over her, his dark eyes seeming to penetrate deep inside her, searching for something. 'About—about last night…' she managed to say, but hated the way she stumbled over the words. 'What I mean is, did we…? Did anything happen between us?'

The air heated around them, laden with explosive sexual tension, but she couldn't look away, couldn't break the connection which was becoming more intense by the second.

'Trust me, Emma, you'd remember if it had.' A smile lifted his lips and a hint of mischief sparked in his eyes.

He was making fun of her.

'Oh,' she said softly, heat infusing her cheeks.

'You sound as if you're disappointed to discover that we slept in the same bed without having sex.' Like a brooding presence, he towered over her, suffocating the very air she breathed, making her pulse leap wildly. 'It can of course be rectified.'

This time she wasn't able to stop the ragged intake of breath or the shudder of desire. He wanted her. Just as she wanted him. It was like the night in Vladimir all over again. Then she had believed she was giving in to the allure of a powerful sexual attraction for just one night; even though they were to be married, she knew this was exactly that again. He didn't love her. This was nothing more than sex.

Her heart thumped hard, and warnings echoed in her mind, but she didn't want to heed them. She wanted Nikolai, wanted him to desire her, and the allure of that was more powerful than the prophecy of a broken heart.

The seconds ticked by and the power of the sexual chemistry between them increased as surely as if he'd touched her. Her body yearned for his touch, her lips craved his kiss, but most of all she wanted his possession. She wanted to be his.

Nikolai stood over Emma as she sat and looked up at him. Did she have any idea just how damn sexy

she looked in that white vest top, her nipples strain-
ing against the fabric? As for the white shorts, well,
he couldn't go there or he'd drag her off to his room
like a Neanderthal.

'We could rectify it now—tonight.' The lust coursing through him had got the better of him, and he spoke
the words before he had time to think, but, judging by
the sexy, impish smile, it wasn't something she was
horrified by.

'Could we?' Her voice was husky, teasing him and
testing him. Damn it. What was the point in denying
the attraction which fizzed around them? He wanted
her and, unless he was very much mistaken, she wanted
him too.

'I want you, Emma,' he said and held out his hand
to her, more emotionally exposed than he'd ever been
in his life. He had no idea how, but this woman was
dismantling every barrier he'd erected to shut himself
away, to prevent himself from ever having to feel anything for anyone.

The silky softness of her throat moved as she swallowed, her gaze fixed on his. Then she parted her lips,
the small movement so sexy he almost groaned out
loud. Finally she took his hand, placing hers in his,
and he pulled her gently to her feet and towards him.

Shock rocked through him as her body collided with
his and he wrapped his arms around her, pulling her
against him. Her body seemed to beg his for more, but
he wanted to hear it from her lips, needed to know this
was what she wanted. 'Is this what you want?'

She slipped from his embrace and he drew in a sharp
breath as she crossed her arms in front of her and, taking hold of her vest top and pulling it over her head,

threw it carelessly to the floor. His gaze devoured her slender figure, her full breasts, and he clenched his hands into tight fists as he fought to hold on to control. But when she slithered the white shorts down her legs, kicking them aside, he knew that control was fading fast.

It was like Vladimir all over again. Except this time he didn't have to worry about consequences. This time he could make her his totally.

'Yes.' That one word was a husky whisper that sent fire all over him at the knowledge this woman was his, and the fact that she'd given him her virginity only increased the power of that idea.

He closed his eyes briefly against the need to take her quickly, to thrust into her and possess her more completely than he had ever taken a woman before. She'd only ever known his touch and because of that he had to take it slowly, make this a night of pure pleasure for both of them.

Slowly he undid his jeans, maintaining eye contact with her as he removed them to stand before her as naked as she was. A dart of satisfied pleasure zipped through him as she lowered her gaze to look at him, arousing him still further.

She moved back to him, looking into his eyes and taking on the role of seductress, just as she had in Vladimir; she wrapped her fingers around him, pushing him to a new level of control. He actually trembled with the pleasure of her touch and groaned as her lips pressed against his, her hand still working the magic.

When she let go of him and kissed down his neck, over his chest, he groaned in pleasure, but when she lowered herself down to continue the torture her touch had started it was nearly his undoing. He pushed his fingers deep into her hair but, as his control began to slip, he pulled her back and she looked up at him, her green eyes dark and full of question.

'My turn.' The gravelly growl of his voice was almost unrecognisable as he pulled her to her feet then pushed her back onto the sofa. With predatory instinct he knelt up before her and, leaning on her, pressed his lips to hers, taking in her gasp of pleasure.

'Nikolai,' she breathed as he kissed down her neck rapidly. She arched herself towards him as he took one nipple between his teeth, nipping, teasing, before caressing it with his tongue.

Again enforced restraint made him shake and he braced his arms tighter to hold himself over her. She writhed in pleasure beneath him as he turned his attention to the other nipple, her hands roaming hungrily over his body.

As he moved lower still, kissing over her stomach, she clutched at his shoulders, her nails digging in, the spike of pain so erotic he could hardly hang on to his control any longer. But he wasn't finished with her yet.

He moved his head between her legs, tasting her as she lifted her hips upwards, all but begging him for more. He teased her with his tongue, pushing her to the edge, but stopping as he felt her begin to tremble, not ready to let her go over just yet.

'Let's go to the bedroom,' he said between kisses as he moved back up over her stomach, over the hardened peak of her nipple and up her throat.

'No,' she gasped as she clung to him, wrapping her legs around him, the heat of her touching him; he knew that he was lost, that all control was gone.

In one swift move he filled her, thrusting deep into her and making her his once more. She gasped as she gripped harder onto his back, her hips lifting to take him deeper inside her. It was wild. Passionate.

Her body was hot and damp against his, but still it wasn't enough. He wanted more, much more. With a growl he thrust harder, striking up a fierce rhythm she matched. Her cries of pleasure pushed him further until he forgot everything except her. With one final thrust, he took her over the edge with him.

Darkness still filled the room as Emma lay contentedly against Nikolai after the hours of making love. They had moved from the sofa to the shower and then finally to his bed. She should be exhausted, but she'd never been so alive, so vibrant. It was almost too good to be true.

The doubts she'd had about accepting his so-called proposal had been blown away by the hot sex they'd shared. If things were that good between them, wasn't there hope he might one day feel something deeper for her? She certainly wanted that to be true because her feelings were definitely growing for him. They had become deep and meaningful. Did that mean she was falling in love with him?

As the question reared up before her, Nikolai stirred and she braced herself, remembering how she'd woken to find him staring out of the window in Vladimir. Had he regretted that night? A night which had changed both of their lives beyond recognition. More questions stirred in her mind as Nikolai propped himself up on his elbow and looked at her, his eyes filling with desire once more.

'I'm going to see some sights today,' she said, trying to fight the rise of a fresh wave of desire. She didn't want their time together to be all about sex. She wanted to get to know him better, but while he kept the barrier raised around himself that was going to be difficult. Did he ever let anyone get close?

'We'll go together.' He pulled her against him and kissed her and she almost gave in.

'That would be nice,' she said with a teasing smile and moved away from him. 'It will be a nice way to get to know each other better.'

'How much better do we need to know each other?' He was smiling but there was a hint of caution in his voice.

'There's so much we don't know about each other.'

'Such as?' The hard tone of his voice had become guarded and it was like being back in Vladimir that first night with him. The impenetrable wall was right round him, shutting her out.

'What we really want from this marriage.' She let the words fall softly between them.

'I know what you want. You want financial security. Why else would you come all this way? You also want for your child what you never had—a father figure.'

Did he have any idea he'd got it so right? Was he really that cruel he'd manipulate her insecurities so coldly?

'My offer of marriage is exactly what you wanted.' He spoke again and all she could do was take it, knowing it was all true. 'Even though you held out for a bit more, marriage is what you came here for, wasn't it, Emma?'

'What?' She couldn't believe what he was saying,

but neither could she move. All she could do was stay there and look at him.

'Is tonight part of a bigger plan?'

How could a night so perfect turn into a one so terrible? Emma shivered in the shadow of the gulf which had opened up between them at the mention of the deal they'd struck. 'Is that what you really think?'

'You have given me no reason to think otherwise.' He threw back the sheets and strode across the room to pull on his jeans, totally uncaring about his nakedness. He was running again.

'Nikolai.' She said his name more sharply than she intended. 'Don't go. Not again.'

He stood at the end of the bed in the semi-darkness of the room and glared at her. 'What exactly is it you want to know, Emma? And, more to the point, who is asking—the woman I am to marry, the one who is carrying my child or the woman who wants to get to the truth just for an article in a magazine?'

Emma recoiled at his fierce tone, but it proved he was hiding the truth, that whatever it was he'd gone to great lengths to conceal from her in Vladimir was still there, creating a barrier around him as physical as a wall of bricks and mortar.

'I'm asking, Nikolai—as your fiancée—because I care, because if we don't deal with this, whatever it is that's keeping you emotionally shut away, making you so cold, it will fester between us, always dominating, always threatening. Do you want your child to grow up under that cloud?' Her passionate plea didn't dent his armour.

'What do you want? My life story? I gave you that in Vladimir.'

'You gave me the version you wanted me to know, but things have changed. We are having a baby and, if we're to marry, then I want that marriage to be a success. I don't want our child to grow up knowing any kind of insecurities.'

'What do you know of insecurities, Emma?' His voice had softened, taken on a more resigned tone.

'Much more than you might think.' Her own childhood, the unhappiness of continuously moving to new foster homes, crept back to the fore, as did her father's rejection. She pushed it away. Nikolai must never know what sort of mother she'd been raised by. If he did, he might think she wasn't fit to be a mother herself, and she couldn't risk her baby being taken away, like she and Jess had been.

'Do you really think that's possible?' He glared at her and she knew he was angry that she was not only challenging him but being evasive herself.

'Tell me, Nikolai. I know some of your story but, as your fiancée, I want to hear it from you.' She spoke softly and held her breath as he paced the room and ran his fingers quickly through his hair.

Nikolai didn't know where to start. He was angry, at himself and Emma. She knew the basic facts so why did she want more? He looked down into her eyes and realised it didn't matter any more what he tried to keep from her; she knew half the story and he was sure that it would only be a matter of time before she'd know every sordid detail. Better it came from him—now.

'Why exactly do you feel it is necessary to know?' Why the hell was he doing this? It was far too deep, too emotionally exposing, and he just didn't do emotion. He'd learnt long ago how to keep fear, anger and even love out of whatever he was doing. Each time he'd come to his mother's rescue as his father had used his fists, he'd acted calmly and without emotion. It hadn't mattered whether he was wiping her bleeding nose or merely standing between them, he'd been devoid of any emotion. It had been the only way—and still was.

'You said before, in Vladimir, that your parents were forced to marry.' She nudged his memory with the start of the story he'd told her that night they'd first slept together. Then, just as now, being with her had threatened to unleash his emotions.

'Yes, they were, but only because she was pregnant with his child.' He watched her face pale and had the urge to kiss her, to forget the past and lose himself in her wonderful body once more. It surged through him like a madness. Thankfully, sense prevailed. Despite the fact that she looked so sexy sitting there naked in his bed, her hair no longer sleek but ruffled from sex, he was sufficiently in control to acknowledge things were already complicated enough without giving her hope of having a normal, loving marriage.

'That's hardly the crime of the century,' she said, sympathy in her voice and a smile lingering tentatively on her lips as he sat on the bed and looked at her.

He knew what she meant. She was pregnant with his child and they were going to be married; that fact only compounded his misgivings, making him ever more determined to keep emotions out of this deal they'd struck, because that was how he had to think of it: as a deal for his child. Just as his father had forced his mother into marriage, he was forcing her.

Now the one thing he didn't want to happen was

happening. Emotions were clamouring from his childhood, demanding to be felt, and he hated it. Memories rushed back at him and he fought for control. What would she think of him if she knew the truth?

He should just say it. However he tried to dress it up, those words would be painful; knowing how he'd come into the world, how it had forced his mother into something she hadn't wanted, made him feel worthless. It was that sense of worthlessness which had driven him hard, making everything he did a success.

He looked at Emma and knew she had to know just who he was.

'He'd raped her.'

There, he'd said it. Finally said the words aloud. He was the unwanted product of a rape which had devastated his mother's life, forcing her into a violent marriage.

'Rape?' Her voice was hardly more than a whisper, and it helped to be near the warmth of her body as the cold admission finally came out, but strangely just saying those words wasn't enough. He wanted to tell it all now he'd finally started, as if he'd opened a door he could never close.

'My father was a family friend and had asked to marry my mother. He'd wanted the connections our family name and wealth would bring him.'

Emma didn't say anything but moved a little closer to him, heat from her body infusing him. He wanted to hold her, to feel the goodness within her cleanse the badness from him, but he couldn't, not yet, not until she knew it all. 'Did she refuse him?'

He gritted his teeth as he recalled the time he'd first found out what had happened, how his gentle and loving mother had become the wife of a vicious brute of a man just because of him. He had no idea why, but now he wanted to talk, to tell Emma everything, even knowing she could use it all and destroy him. He wanted to prevent it all coming out as a headline story in the press. That was why he'd flown from New York to a country he barely remembered to ensure a grandmother he'd come to hate didn't tell her the damned story. Now here he was, spilling it all out to the very woman who wanted to know his family story for that very reason.

'She did. And because of that he attacked and raped her.' He bit down on the anger which raged in him now, just as it had done the day he'd realised he'd been the reason his mother had married a violent man. Surely their life would have been better without a man like that in it? He'd never questioned his mother, never asked her about it. She didn't even know he'd overheard her and his stepfather talking. That would break her heart as much as the story being leaked to the world would.

'I don't understand. Why did she marry him after that?' Incredulity filled her voice as she once again looked up at him.

'That is something I have never understood.' Despite the warmth of her body his mind drifted back in time, to the many occasions when he'd cowered in a corner, hiding from his father's wrath. 'When my mother and I left Russia I was ten and I never wanted to go there again. I did all I could to fit in with our new life, to please my new father. It was like being given a new chance.'

'Why did your mother marry your father if he'd done that?' It was a question he'd asked himself so many times.

'Maybe she saw marriage to that brute as her only chance. She was from a well-known family and wouldn't have wanted to bring such a scandal out into the open.'

Emma moved and wrapped her arms around him, pressing her lips to his forehead. It was strangely comforting to be held by her, to feel her compassion wrapping around him. 'I'm sorry,' she whispered. 'For making you go there again.'

'Maybe I should have faced my father's mother when I had the chance, asked her why she helped to hide such horrible things from the world. From the outside we must have appeared a normal family. I want to know if she realises that by doing that she trapped my mother and I with an angry bully. Only his sudden death freed us.'

'It doesn't mean we shall be the same,' she said, homing in on the worry he'd had since the moment she'd arrived in New York with the news of her pregnancy. He wasn't fit to be a father with a past like that, but that just made him more determined to be a part of his child's life, to be a better father.

'How can you say that when you only agreed to marriage for the child's sake?' He began to build his barriers back again, using all the ammunition he had to push her away. As he spoke he looked into her eyes and saw the flash of pain within them, but buried it deep inside him.

'Our child was not conceived through violence,' she said firmly as she touched his face with the palm of her hand, a gesture he wanted to enjoy, but he couldn't allow himself that luxury.

'But it most definitely wasn't conceived out of love.' He threw the harsh truth at her and her hand stilled.

'No, it wasn't.' The softness of her voice, mixed with sadness, slashed at him harshly. What the hell had he been thinking of, talking about this with her?

She moved away from him, looking like a hurt and wounded animal, and that strange sensation squeezed his chest again. This was getting far too deep for him and he had to put a stop to it right now.

'I never want to talk of this again.' Anger boiled over inside him, threatening to spill out everywhere, turn him into a copy of the man who'd terrified him as a child, and she'd done that to him.

Emma looked up at him and he watched her bare shoulders go back as she sat a little taller, her chin lifting in that sexily defiant way of hers. 'I understand, and we won't.'

She understood? How could she understand? He wanted to ask her about her childhood, just what it was in her past that qualified her even to say that, but he couldn't deal with any more emotion. He needed space, time on his own. He strode from the bedroom as the light of dawn filled the apartment, thankful that she hadn't attempted to follow or ask anything else.

CHAPTER NINE

THE GENUINE CONCERN Nikolai had been showing her all week, taking time out from the office and going sightseeing with her, had definitely brought them closer in many ways. After the disastrous way last weekend had ended she felt a glimmer of hope and the uneasy sensation that she was doing the wrong thing marrying him melted into the background.

Today he'd chosen a trip on the Hudson River to see the Statue of Liberty. He'd hired a private boat and it was so romantic it reinstated the flailing hope. It was a perfect spring day but, even so, the motion of the boat was making her queasy. Just as she had done every day this week, she tried to hide it from him but, as if he'd become tuned into her feelings, he guessed she was unwell.

'This wasn't such a good idea,' he said as he stood behind her and pulled her close against him. She closed her eyes, enjoying the sensation of being cared for, being protected. Deep down it was all she'd ever wanted. Love and protection had been so lacking in her childhood it had become the elusive dream. A dream which right at this moment felt tantalisingly close.

'It's fine,' she said as she snuggled closer. The spring

wind not yet carrying any warmth didn't help, but, against the man she was most definitely falling in love with, she really didn't care about anything. Being here in his arms like this was so right, so natural, she didn't want anything to spoil it. 'I just don't think I can take photos today.'

'Then don't.' He kissed the top of her head and she smiled. Was he falling in love with her too? Could she be on the brink of her happy-ever-after? 'You should stop working and just enjoy the moment. Photographs can wait.'

'Can I ask you something?' She started speaking while watching the buildings of New York become ever taller and more modern as they made their way down the river towards downtown Manhattan. Before he had a chance to reply, she spoke again. 'Have you ever been in love?'

She needed to ask, needed to know if he'd ever let a woman into his heart before, but the tension in his arms as he held her warned her she'd gone too far.

'No.' The sharply spoken word told her more than she needed to know. 'You know what happened when I was a child. You even told me yourself that you didn't believe in such nonsense as love.'

'I didn't,' she said softly and swallowed down the disappointment. If his mother had found happiness after such a terrible marriage, then love must exist. Her heart was opening to the idea, but could his?

'I hope that doesn't mean you've changed your mind.' The sharpness of his words cut the air around them and she shivered, as if winter had returned.

Her heart went into freefall and she focused hard on the New York skyline, determined not to allow his throwaway comments to hurt her, but the truth was she had changed her mind. She'd changed it because of her deepening feelings for him, feelings that she knew for sure could only be love.

'Of course I haven't,' she said quickly, sensing that to tell him now wouldn't be sensible. She had to remember why she was here as his fiancée at all. She was carrying his child and he'd made a deal with her, a deal which gave her baby all she'd missed out on as a child, and she wasn't about to jeopardise that. 'We are doing this for our child.'

'And your sister.' His stern reminder left her in no doubt he considered his offer the deal clincher. It was nothing more than a deal for him, but his next words cut her heart in two, making her feel shallow. 'Funds for her "dream", as you called it, were the sealing factor in the deal, were they not?'

He let her go and moved to stand next to her, feigning an interest in the city's skyline, and she knew she'd got too close to the barriers erected around him, barriers to prevent him from being affected by any kind of sentimental feelings. Deep inside her that newly discovered well of hope dried up. She had thought he might be able to find it in his heart to feel something for her, as she was beginning to for him.

They'd created a child together in a night of passion, a child that would bind them together for evermore, but she wanted more than that. She wanted to be loved and love in return. Every night this week, since they'd returned from their engagement party, the hours of darkness had been filled with passion and her love had grown, but for him it had been nothing more than sex.

She'd let herself down, done the one thing he'd

warned her not to do. She wanted more; it hurt to admit it, but she loved him. She tried to distract herself with thoughts of her sister but they made her lonelier than she'd ever been. The last few times she'd called her, Jess hadn't been able to take the call, and she'd just received brief texts in reply.

'I'd like to see if Jess can make it to New York for our wedding.' She tried tentatively to steer the discussion away from the subject of love. Maybe it was a safer thing to talk about. 'Do we have a date yet?'

He laughed softly and looked at her, almost frazzling her resolve not to feel anything for him. 'Are you that keen to become my wife or are you just changing the subject?'

'There's nothing to be gained by waiting now we have agreed our terms.' It might be the truth, but her voice had a tart edge to it as she tried to stem the hurt and rejection growing within her.

He looked at her, studying her face for a few seconds, and all she could hear was the sound of the boat engine and the wash of water. The spring sunshine was warm on her face, but not as searing as his gaze. 'Then you'll be pleased to know it has all been arranged for this Saturday.'

'Saturday?' She whirled round to face him, not caring that she was missing the spectacular views he'd brought her here to see. Saturday was too soon. She'd never be able to organise Jess flying in from Moscow by then. Was he deliberately trying to cut her off from everything she held dear? 'Jess will never be able to get here by Saturday—and she's all I have, Nikolai.'

Before he could answer, her phone rang and she snatched at the chance of avoiding his scrutiny. She'd

left so many messages for Jess, it had to be her, and she
needed to speak to her now more than ever. She looked
at the screen, but it wasn't her sister. It was Richard.
Nikolai looked down at the screen while she thought of
not answering. She didn't need to talk to Richard of all
people right at this moment, no matter how much he'd
helped her get her contract with *World in Photographs*.

'You had better answer that.' His voice was harsh,
each word clipped with anger. She looked up at him
in confusion but he turned from her and walked away
a few paces.

'Richard,' she said as she answered the call. 'How
lovely to hear from you.'

Nikolai didn't like the way Emma smiled as she spoke
to Richard or the way she'd turned her back on him
to take the call. He recalled he was the photographer
who'd helped her get her career off the ground, but
now he was beginning to question exactly what she
thought of him.

'The article is out?' Emma's voice carried across
the deck as she continued her call. 'That's brilliant.
Thanks for calling to tell me—and, Richard, thanks
for your help.'

Nikolai clenched his jaw against the irrational anger
which bubbled up just from hearing her talk to this
other man. Was it really possible that he was jealous?
The thought was ludicrous. To be jealous of another
man he'd have to have feelings for Emma—deep feelings he just didn't want.

He turned to watch her as she spoke on the phone.
Her long silky hair was in a ponytail down her back,
but the wind kept playing with it, reminding him how

it felt against his skin while she slept. For the last week, since the night they had returned from their engagement party, she had spent every night in his bed. Each of those nights of passion had claimed them in its frenzied dance; afterwards she'd always slept wrapped around him and he'd enjoyed the closeness.

Her laughter as she responded to something Richard said only served to send his irritation levels higher and he turned from her, determined he wasn't going to be affected by it. Their marriage was to be one of convenience for the sake of his child and all he had to do was remind himself how easily she'd been talked into the marriage once he'd used the lure of funds for her sister.

Before Richard had called, he'd been about to tell her that he'd made arrangements for Jess to come to New York for the wedding. He'd put things in motion after the engagement party, which had been all about his family and friends, because he'd wanted her to have someone there for her. He'd also insisted that the wedding itself was limited strictly to close family, which had been a battle with his mother, but now the urge to tell her these details had gone.

'That was Richard,' she said as she joined him and he certainly couldn't miss the smile on her face. Irritation surged deeper through him at the happiness in her voice. 'The article is out and he said it's really good.'

'If it's what I have already read, then I am pleased for you.' He kept his voice neutral, not wanting a trace of any kind of emotion to be heard, especially the new and strange one he suddenly had to deal with.

'Why would it be any different?' She frowned up at him. 'You don't trust me, do you, Nikolai?'

Of course he didn't trust her and now, thanks to a

moment of weakness, she knew everything. She still had the ability to shatter his mother's happiness. That was something he wasn't going to allow to happen at any price and precisely why he'd flown to Russia in the first place.

'Is Richard a close friend of yours?' he asked, unable to keep his curiosity under control any longer, or the anger at the way the idea of Richard and Emma being close filled him with such strong emotions.

'Why do you ask?' Her cautious question was just what he'd expected—and feared. She was hiding something; of that he was certain.

Despite his suspicions, there was no way he was going to let her know how he felt, so he assumed an air of indifference he definitely didn't feel. 'I have limited the wedding guests to immediate family and close friends. I just wanted to know if he was a close friend.'

She looked down, not able to meet his gaze, and when she looked up again disappointment and sadness were in her eyes, but he refused to be made to feel guilty. 'He's helped me a lot and, yes, once I hoped we could be more than friends. I'm sure there are women like that in your past.'

He hadn't anticipated such honesty and it threw him off balance for a moment as he realised the truth of what she'd said. 'There was someone once, yes.'

Why had he said that? Why had he brought his ex-fiancée into this?

'Someone you loved?' she asked cautiously.

'No, someone I couldn't love, someone who needed that from me and I couldn't give it to her—or maybe it was because I didn't want to give it. Either way, the engagement ended.'

'You were engaged?' Her brows lifted in surprise and he regretted saying anything, but then maybe it would back up all he'd already told her, convince her that love was not something he could do.

'I was, yes.' He didn't want to have this conversation with her. It was something he never spoke of.

She clutched at her hair and looked away from him, as if she sensed his reluctance to talk. 'I've always wanted to see the Statue of Liberty. Thanks for this.'

Shocked by her change of subject, he looked up, and sure enough they were close to the statue as it reached up into the spring sky. He'd been so absorbed in her and the way he was thinking about her, feeling about her, that he hadn't even registered they'd got this far.

Emma turned and looked at him, her expression serious. What was it about this woman that muddled his senses so much? Every time he was with her he lost all clarity on what it was he wanted from her and from life.

'I don't expect love from you, Nikolai.' Her voice was as clear as a mountain stream but it didn't settle the unease he felt.

'What do you expect?'

'Nothing, Nikolai. You've made that perfectly clear from the very beginning. Our marriage is purely for the baby's sake.' She laid her hand lightly on his arm and, just as he had done before, he pulled back from her touch, not wanting such intimacy.

'We each have things to gain from the marriage, Emma.'

Emma looked at Nikolai and her heart began to break. She knew the whole thing was a deal, that their marriage was nothing more than a convenience, but always there had been a spark of hope fuelled by the heady passion they'd shared. Now that spark had gone, extinguished by his cold words.

'All I want is to be able to bring up my child, Nikolai. Do you promise me my ability to do that will never be questioned, even if we are apart?' She didn't want to tell him the truth behind her demands, but if it made him realise just how much she wanted this then it would have to be done.

She wanted her child to know who she was, not to think of her as a distant shadow in the background, as her own mother had become. It still hurt that a woman could turn her back so easily on the two children she'd given birth to, but she'd always told herself and Jess that their mother had been sick and didn't know what she was doing. Now, with her own baby on the way, she seriously doubted this. Her mother just hadn't wanted either her or Jess.

Nikolai's dark eyes searched hers but she couldn't look into them for fear he'd see the pain she felt about her mother and she looked beyond him to the passing city as the boat headed back along the river to the pier they'd left earlier.

'Why would I ever question that?' He moved a little closer, as if sensing there was much more to her demand.

She looked back at him, feeling the cooling wind in her face. 'I have already told you my sister and I were in care as children.'

He frowned and looked down at her, his mouth set in a firm line of annoyance. She was well aware now that he hated personal conversations, anything that meant he might have to connect emotionally. Did he think she was trying to make him feel sorry for her?

Before he could say anything which might stop the flow of words from her, she continued. Whatever he thought, this was something that had to be told. She couldn't spend the rest of her life, whether living with Nikolai or not, worried that she might be classed as an unfit mother and her child taken from her. She knew what it felt like to be that child.

'We were taken into care because my mother couldn't look after us. She'd rather have cuddled a bottle of something strong and alcoholic than hold my sister, and certainly hadn't worried about me.'

She looked directly at the passing buildings, into the mass of stone and windows that created a maze that ordinarily she'd long to explore. Now it was just something to look at. She couldn't look at Nikolai, didn't want to see the disapproval on his face. All she wanted was the promise that, no matter what happened between them, she could be a mother to her child.

'Do you really think I would keep a mother and child apart?' The stinging anger in his voice forced her to turn and look at him, and his dark eyes sparked with annoyance, heightening her own sense of anxiety.

'You made it virtually impossible for me to refuse the marriage deal.' Had he forgotten how he'd dominated that discussion?

'You were the one who quickly accepted the suggestion of funds for your sister.'

'It wasn't exactly a suggestion, Nikolai. It was more of a demand. It probably even comes much closer to blackmail.' She should tell him about her father, about the fear and rejection she'd grown up with.

Darkness clouded his eyes, as if the spring sun had slipped behind a cloud. 'It was not a demand and most certainly not blackmail. What kind of man do you think I am that I need to use such underhanded tactics?'

Defiantly she looked up into the icy blackness of his eyes. Her heart was pounding in her chest but she knew this had to be dealt with before they married. She didn't want to enter into a marriage, even a loveless one, with unresolved issues such as these. She couldn't live with that uncertainty hanging over her.

'I don't know, Nikolai. You have made it clear marriage isn't something you want to enter into freely, and yet you insist your mother lives under the illusion that we are in love. What kind of man does that make you?'

'I want only the best for my child. That's what kind of man I am.'

The boat bumped against the pier and Nikolai looked at Emma, wondering just what kind of monster she thought he was. Did she really believe he would separate her and their child, after all he'd told her about his childhood? Anger rushed through him and he couldn't look at her any more, couldn't take the accusation in her eyes.

Had he made a mistake, insisting on marriage? He couldn't walk away from his child, but none of this felt right.

No, it had to be this way. It was the only way he could prove he was not like his father, that despite the genes inside him he had his mother's goodness, he could be a good father. He wanted his son or daughter's childhood to be very different from what he'd known—and from what Emma had known, if what she'd told him was anything to go by.

'Do you really believe a loveless marriage is the way to achieve that?' she demanded hotly.

Her question caught him off guard and neither of them moved, despite the need to leave the boat. That word again. Why did love have to come into everything?

'Our marriage will achieve that precisely because it won't be swallowed up by nonsense such as love.' The hardness of his tone shocked her; he could see it in her eyes, feel it radiating off her.

'And what if one of us falls in love?' Her bold question challenged him from every side. Nikolai's suspicion about the ever-helpful Richard increased.

'If what you told me before is true, that will not happen. Neither of us believe in love—unless of course you are already in love with another man?' Again that irrational jealousy seeped into him as he thought of how happy she'd been talking to Richard on the phone. How she'd smiled and laughed.

'How can I love another man when I have known only you?' The hurt in her voice was clear, but his rational sense had jumped ship, replacing it with intense jealousy for a man he hadn't even met. A man who could make *his* fiancée smile so brightly that happiness danced in her eyes.

'Do you love Richard?' He couldn't think clearly, and didn't even register her words properly, but fired the question at her. She gasped in shock and stepped back from him.

'You think I am in love with Richard?'

'Why is that so implausible?' Impatience filled him at her act of innocence. She'd used that act once before.

'Because he's a friend. But I'll be honest with you—

it hurts like hell to feel anything for someone who feels nothing for you. But you wouldn't know what that's like, would you, Nikolai?'

Before he had a chance to ask more, she left him standing on the deck and he watched as she disembarked and strode away from him. What the hell had all that meant?

CHAPTER TEN

EMMA HAD TRIED to keep alive the flicker of hope that things had changed between them after returning from their engagement party. Nikolai had avoided the painful discussion they'd had that night, but had played to perfection the role of adoring fiancé. Yesterday on the boat had doused that hope and now the ever-increasing nausea was making everything so much more difficult to deal with.

'I've cleared the diary for today,' he said as he strode across the room to stand looking, brooding, out over the park and the vastness of New York beyond. His withdrawal from her made her feel insignificant and rejected, feeding into her childhood insecurities which were growing by the day.

'You did that yesterday; please don't feel you have to do it again.' A wave of nausea washed over her. She pressed her hand against her forehead, her elbow on her lap, and curled over as a sharp pain shot through her. She didn't feel well enough to do anything this morning, least of all play happy bride-to-be with Nikolai.

Was it the strain of everything: the way he'd manipulated the whole marriage deal, using the one thing she wouldn't wish upon any child, least of all her own?

Another cramp caused her to take in a sharp breath and she bit down against the pain. There was something wrong. Very wrong. Panic rushed through her like a river breaking over a waterfall. She wanted this baby so much, with or without Nikolai's support, but what was happening to her? What had she done wrong?

'Nikolai,' she said, her voice shaky. 'The baby. Something's wrong.'

She closed her eyes against another wave of nausea and tried to fight back the tears—not just tears of pain, but tears of fear for her baby. She couldn't take it if something happened. What if she lost her baby? In the back of her mind, as the fog of pain increased, the thought that it was exactly what Nikolai would want rampaged round like a wild animal, making her angry and more panicked.

'Emma.' Nikolai's stern voice snapped her back from that fog and she looked up at him as he stood over her, phone in hand. His brows were snapped together in worry and his face set hard in stern lines. 'I'm taking you to the hospital.'

A tear slid down her cheek as relief washed over her. He was in control. But could he stop what was happening, what she feared was the worst thing possible? As another pain stabbed at her stomach she closed her eyes and the need to give in to the blackness rushing around her was too much. Would that be the best thing to do for the baby? Further questions were silenced as she let go and did exactly that.

When she opened her eyes again she knew she was in hospital and panic charged over her like a herd of wild, stampeding horses. She tried to sit up, but Nikolai's hand pressed into her shoulder, preventing her from doing so. 'It's okay. Lie still.'

His voice was soothing and commanding without any of the panic she felt, but still she tried to get up. She wanted answers, wanted to know what was happening to her and her baby.

'My baby?'

He leant over her, forcing her to look into his face, his eyes. She smelt his aftershave, felt the warmth of his hand on her shoulder, and relished the calm control he had. 'The baby is fine. You are fine. So please, just relax. Stress won't help you or the baby at all.'

'Thank goodness.' She breathed and closed her eyes as relief washed over her.

What would she have done if she had lost the baby? A terrible thought entered her mind, slipping in like an unwanted viper. If this had happened just a week later, and it had had the most unthinkable consequences, she and Nikolai would have been married. What would he have done then, married to a woman who no longer carried the child he'd made a deal for?

'You have been doing too much,' he said sternly. 'Rest is what you need.'

'Maybe we should call off the wedding.' She couldn't look at him, couldn't bear to see the truth in his eyes. She'd been rejected by her father before he'd even seen her and then again as a teenager. For him marriage and fatherhood wasn't what he'd wanted in life and she knew it was the same for Nikolai; he'd made that more than clear. She couldn't trap him into something he didn't want but neither could she deny her baby the chance of knowing its father. A heart-wrenching decision, born out of the panic of the moment, grew in her mind. Who should she be true to—her child or herself?

'If the doctor agrees you are well and can come home, that will not happen.' There wasn't a drop of gentleness in his voice. The man who'd become more gentle and loving each night had gone and the cold, hard man who'd walked out on her in Vladimir was back.

'But this isn't what you want.' She hated the pain that sounded in her voice, hated the way she still clung to the hope he could one day love her.

'What we want is irrelevant.' He looked down at her, his dark eyes narrowed with irritation. 'It's what is best for the child, Emma. We will be married.'

Nikolai fought hard against the invading emotions as he helped Emma to sit up. This was more than the physical pull of sexual attraction that had surrounded them since the day they'd first met in Vladimir. This was something he'd never known before. Something he'd been running from since the night he'd made her his.

He cared, really cared, not just about the child who was his heir but about the woman he'd created that child with. When had that happened? When had lust and sexual desire crossed the divide and become something deeper, something much more powerful than passion?

He had no idea when, but all he knew was that it had happened. He looked down at Emma, her face full of uncertainty, and knew without doubt that he cared for her. And it scared the hell out of him. Caring caused pain.

'We will take Emma for a scan now.' The nurse's

voice snapped him back from that daunting revelation. A scan? Would he be able to see his child? Now?

'Is there something wrong?' The quiver in Emma's voice reached into his heart and pulled at it, making him want to hold her hand, give her reassurance. Making him want to love her. But how could he do that when he didn't know how to deal with the emotions that were taking over? Or even exactly what they were?

'Is there?' he demanded of the nurse.

'Everything is fine,' she said with the kind of smile meant to dispel any doubts. 'We just want to reassure both of you.'

'Thank you.' Emma's reply called his attention back to her and he looked down at her, noticing, as he had done several times in recent days, how pale she was. Should he have done something sooner? Guilt ploughed into him. He'd pushed her too hard, not taken enough interest to see how tired she'd become. He'd risked his baby.

His baby.

Those two words crashed into him and for a moment he couldn't draw a breath. Then he felt Emma's hand on his arm, the sympathetic touch almost too much. He didn't deserve that from her.

A short time later, and with no recollection of how he'd got there, he was in a small room with Emma. She lay on the bed, the soft skin of her stomach exposed as the nurse pressed the scanner probe against her. He noticed her hand was clenched as it held her top out of the way, as if she feared the worst. He watched as the nurse moved the probe, trying to get a clear image on the screen. He wouldn't have been able to tell Emma was pregnant with his child, her stomach was flat, but the first image filled the screen and he knew the machine didn't lie.

In his mind he tried to add up how many weeks' pregnant she was. How many weeks was it since they'd had the most amazing night which had had such far-reaching consequences. Before he could work it out, the nurse's voice broke through his thoughts.

'There we are. Baby at ten weeks.'

He looked at the screen, not able to take his eyes from it. The fuzzy image had a dark centre and in that darkness was his baby. Small, but unmistakable. He couldn't move, couldn't do anything but stare at it.

A tense silence filled the room as the nurse continued to move the scanner around, losing the image briefly. He couldn't look at Emma, couldn't take his attention away from the screen that showed him the secret of his baby.

'And everything appears normal,' the nurse added as she paused once more, showing an even clearer image. 'See it moving and its heart beating?'

Fierce protectiveness rose up in him like a rearing horse and he knew in that tension-filled moment he would do absolutely anything for his baby. He would go to the ends of the earth for him or her. It would want for nothing and he would love it unconditionally.

Love.

Could he love it? Could he give it the one thing his father had never given him? The one thing which terrified him?

Finally he looked at Emma as she watched the screen, a small tear slipping down her cheek. Did he love her? What was the powerful sensation of crushing around his chest and the lightness in his stomach each time he saw her or thought of her? Was it love? Had he fallen in love with a woman who could never love him? A woman whose heart was already elsewhere?

Emma looked at the screen and tears began to slide down her cheeks. They were in part tears of happiness: her baby was well. She'd seen it move, seen its little heart beating. But those tears of happiness mingled with tears of pain. Nikolai had been silent throughout. He hadn't uttered a word, had barely moved, and she could no longer look at him. Was he now seeing the reality of the deal he'd made?

She glanced up at him now as the nurse completed the scan and then left them alone. No doubt she thought she was giving them private time to be happy together, but then she didn't know the truth.

The truth was that Nikolai didn't want this baby. He'd stood stiffly by her side, his hard gaze fixed rigidly on the screen as the first images of their child had appeared. Now he couldn't move, couldn't look her in the eye.

The elation that filled her from seeing the baby, from knowing it was well, cooled as the tension in the room grew to ominous levels and she wished the nurse hadn't left. At least then she might have been able to avoid the truth.

'You must rest,' Nikolai said, his voice deeper and more commanding than she'd ever known it. Was he blaming her? Was he even now thinking she was as uncaring as her mother had been?

'I—I think we should at least postpone the wedding.' She stumbled over her words as his fiercely intense gaze locked with hers. If she could get him to agree to postpone it then it would give them both time to decide if it really was the right thing to do. She loved him but couldn't marry him, tie him to her, if there was never going to be a chance that he would one day feel the same for her.

'No, but you won't need to worry about anything. I will arrange for your final dress fittings to be at the apartment.'

He moved away as she sat up and slipped off the bed, but she felt more exposed than she had that morning she'd first woken in his bed. It was as if he knew everything about her. She knew he didn't, knew that she still guarded her fear of rejection—his rejection. Her father had rejected her. Richard had too, just by refusing to see her as anything other than a friend, and the last thing she wanted was to be rejected by the father of her baby, the man she'd fallen in love with.

'I'm not sure marriage is the right thing for us at the moment.' It was like standing on the shore, allowing the waves to wash over her toes, each wave taking her deeper into the conversation until it was swim or allow the depths to swallow her up.

His eyes narrowed. 'Why?'

'It doesn't feel right, Nikolai.'

'We made a deal, Emma.' The uncompromising hardness of his voice shocked her.

'It's almost as if you've bought me, bought the baby.'

'You agreed to the deal, Emma, and if my memory serves me right held out for just that little bit more. Not content with securing yours and the baby's future, you also wanted to secure your sister's.'

'But this isn't right. We don't love each other.' The plea in her voice must have reached him somehow because he moved closer to her and she waited with bated breath to see what he was going to do or say.

'Love isn't always needed, Emma.' He touched her cheek, brushing his fingers across her skin so softly she could almost imagine he cared. 'Sometimes passion and desire is a better base on which to build a marriage and we've proved many times that exists between us.'

'But that's not love, Nikolai.' She drew in a shuddering breath as he moved even closer. Why couldn't he just admit he didn't love her, that he would never feel that for her?

'I don't care what it is, we made our deal with it.'

'But will it be enough?' She stepped away from him, wanting to get out of this dimly lit room and away from the sudden intensity in his eyes.

Nikolai looked at Emma as she tried to evade him. Was she that desperate to get away from him? Was he doing the right thing, insisting the marriage deal went ahead?

'For me, yes.' There was no way he was going to reveal the depths of the emotions seeing his baby had unlocked. He wanted to protect his child, always be there for it. He also wanted to do the same for Emma, but after the call from Richard he doubted Emma felt the same way.

She'd come to New York to secure her and her child's futures. She must have done her homework on him because she'd then held out for more than that when all he'd wanted was to keep his child in his life.

Fatherhood might not be something he'd looked for, or even wanted, but now that it had happened he wasn't about to let any man or woman stand in the way and prevent him from being a father. He had to prove to himself he had not inherited his father's mean streak.

'And what if one day that changes?' She challenged him further, deepening his resolve to make it work, to be the father he'd never had.

'It will not change, Emma. We have created a child together and that will bind us for all eternity; nothing can change that now.' The truth of his words sounded round in his head and he knew he couldn't let her walk away from their marriage, their deal.

'So there's no going back?' An obstinate strength sounded in her voice, as if sparring with him was making her stronger.

'Never.'

CHAPTER ELEVEN

THERE WERE JUST two more days until she married Nikolai and Emma was restless. She'd been taking it easy since returning from the hospital but today felt different. She'd had lots of time to think and, although Emma knew brides had nerves, she didn't think they had the serious doubts she was being plagued with.

She still cringed with embarrassment at how close she'd come to revealing she loved him whilst they were on the boat, but those tense few minutes in the hospital had highlighted how bad the idea of marrying him was.

His reaction at the scan emphasised clearly that marriage was the wrong thing to do. She could feel him pulling away from her emotionally, locking down those barriers again, and she braced herself for his rejection.

It didn't matter how many times she let the question wage a battle in her mind, she still came back to the same answer: how could she marry a man who didn't love her? Each and every day she had fallen deeper in love. If only they hadn't spent that night together after they'd returned from the party. If only he hadn't stirred her emotions up and awakened her love for him, then maybe she could have merely acted the part of adoring and caring fiancée. Such thoughts were useless when each night spent with him filled her heart with more love.

Her phone bleeped on the table and she abandoned the view of the park she often contemplated and opened the usual daily text from Jess, missing her more than she thought possible. If Jess were here, sharing this moment with her, she might be able to deal with it better.

With a sigh she picked up the phone and read the text from Jess. As she read the words, her heart leapt with excitement.

Surprise! Be with you in five minutes.

Jess was here? In New York? How had that happened? She recalled the lighter conversations with Nikolai when they'd taken the boat along the river. He must have arranged for Jess to come over for their wedding. Why had he done that? He confused her. Such actions made him look nice, as if he did have some feelings for her, making everything even harder. She couldn't back out of the marriage now if Jess was here, knowing that by doing so she'd be letting Jess's chance of a worry-free future slip away as well as depriving her child of its father.

Ignoring the inner churning of her heart, she sent a text back to Jess. Excitement almost took over the nauseating worry that filled her. She wondered again about Nikolai's motives for organising it. With a huff of frustration, she sent a text to Nikolai to say thank you. Two could play at the relationship game.

Before Emma had a chance to do anything else, the apartment door opened and Jess stood there, a big smile on her face. Disbelief kept Emma rooted to the spot for a moment and emotions overwhelmed her. Jess let go of her case and walked towards her and, as she'd always done, Emma enveloped her in a hug, not able to believe she was actually here.

'How did you get here?' she asked when they'd finally let each other go.

'Your wonderful fiancé.' Jess's excitement was palpable and Emma couldn't even think straight. Of course she would think he was so wonderful; it was exactly what she'd wanted her to think. She couldn't let Jess know the real reason she'd accepted the marriage.

'Nikolai?' she asked and Jess laughed.

'How many do you have? Of course Nikolai.' Jess walked around the apartment, taking in the luxury of it all, something neither of them were used to. 'He arranged everything, right down to the key to get in. He's amazing, Em, you're so lucky. He must love you so much.'

Jess's enthusiasm for her soon-to-be brother-in-law was so zealous it almost brought Emma's world crashing down. Despite the miles that had separated them, he'd charmed Jess, made her see what he wanted the rest of the world to see. She'd never felt more trapped in her life.

'He didn't tell me, though,' she said, quickly pushing away the doubts, not wanting them to creep in and spoil this time with Jess.

'Because he wanted to surprise you. He made me promise not to say a word. Have you any idea how hard that's been the last few weeks, keeping it a secret from you?'

Last few weeks? He'd organised this long before they had the discussion about Jess attending the wedding? Had he done it even before their engagement party? Was that why he'd been so concerned that she had nobody there for her that night?

'Well, he's certainly done that,' she said as she took Jess off to her room, determined not to let Nikolai's motives spoil this unexpected moment with her sister.

Nikolai arrived back at his apartment to the sound of women's voices drifting through the open plan living area from the bedroom Emma had used on her arrival, which her sister would now use. For a moment he was taken aback and stood listening to them, grateful that Jess had managed to keep her arrival a secret. The lack of anyone for Emma at their engagement party had made such a surprise important, but the visit to the hospital had reinforced it.

'You're having his baby?' Jess's unfamiliar voice was filled with shock and he remained silent and still, waiting to hear Emma's reply, but none came. Was she smiling and nodding her confirmation to her sister or giving away the truth of it all? Would she let Jess know this was nothing more than a marriage of convenience?

Silence echoed around the apartment for what seemed like hours, but he knew it was merely seconds. He stood still, not daring to move, not wanting them to hear his footsteps on the polished wooden floor. Finally the silence was broken by Jess's voice.

'But you love him, right?' Jess asked, concern in her voice, and Nikolai held his breath, hoping Emma would act the same part she'd acted for his mother, that of a woman in love.

'He's a good man.' Emma's subdued answer was not at all what he'd expected her to say. It seemed her

acting skills were not on form today and disappointment flooded through him. The last thing he wanted
was Emma's younger sister letting slip to his mother
that the marriage was not a love match. That would
make his mother feel guilty for what had happened in
his childhood. The only thing she'd ever wanted was
for him to find the real love she had.

'I thought you wanted true love.' Jess's voice lowered so he was hardly able to hear it and right now he
certainly didn't want to hear Emma's answer. He recalled her light-hearted view on love when they'd first
met and knew it must have been true and not the throwaway comment she'd allowed him to think it was. She
did believe in love, and was looking for it, but love was
something he couldn't give her.

He strode across the room, his footsteps loud on the
polished floor, and perfect for blocking out the answer
he didn't want to hear. He poured himself a much-
needed glass of brandy. The voices had gone silent
and now he wished he had waited to find out what she
thought. Would it be so bad to be loved by the woman
who was carrying his child, his heir? Somewhere deep
inside him the idea stirred those emotions from the day
at the hospital and for a brief moment of madness he
wanted exactly that.

'I didn't hear you come in.' Emma's voice sounded
cautiously behind him and he turned his back on the
view to face her. She looked pale and he wondered if
she was well enough to have Jess here.

'I've only just arrived,' he said grimly, wishing she
didn't have such an effect on him. With just one ques-
tioning look she cracked the defensive shield around

him, made him feel emotions, which as far as he was concerned was dangerous.

She walked closer to him and, for the first time since they'd arrived back from their engagement party, she looked shy and unable to meet his gaze. She'd had the same look in her eyes as she'd met him in the hotel lounge the night after the sleigh ride. That shyness hadn't lasted long. It had soon been replaced by the temptation of a seductress. Had it been that which had pushed his limits of control beyond endurance?

'Thank you,' she said softly.

'For what?' She looked at him with big green eyes and to see the emotion within them was too much. He didn't want the complication of emotion in his life. Never. It was why he hadn't looked at her as they'd seen their baby on the scan.

She smiled shyly. 'For getting Jess here. You have no idea how much that means to me—and Jess.'

As she said the words a young, dark-haired girl came into the room and smiled, the similarities between the sisters striking. 'And you must be Jess?'

Emma turned round as he spoke and held out her hand to her sister. 'We are both grateful for everything, but this is such a surprise. Getting married will be easier with Jess at my side.'

Irritation surged through him. She thought getting married to him was going to be difficult? From what she'd just said, it was obvious Jess was in full possession of the facts; no pretence at love for her sister's benefit was needed now. Didn't that show she was as cold and calculating as he was? It certainly proved she was only marrying him because of the baby.

'You helped me with my mother. It was only fair you got something out of our deal too.' He then turned his attention to Jess, needing to put some barriers back up between him and Emma, uncomfortable at the effect she was having on him. 'Did you have a good flight?'

'I did, thanks. I've never flown first class before,' Jess replied, grinning enthusiastically. He felt Emma's curious gaze on him, but ignored it, and the way his body warmed just from her nearness. He had to get out of here now.

'I'll leave you two girls to it, then. You have dress fittings later.' Before Emma could say or do anything, he left them alone. It was more than obvious to him now that he had to leave and check into a hotel until his wedding day. His wedding day. After ending his first engagement, he'd never thought he'd ever get married, let alone be a father.

He turned at the door. 'I've booked into a hotel until after the wedding, so you will not be disturbed by my presence.'

'You don't have to do that,' Emma said, alarm in her voice.

'Of course he does,' Jess chipped in. 'It's bad luck to see each other before the wedding.'

'In that case, I will go now.'

Emma watched Nikolai leave, angry that after all she'd done for the benefit of his mother he'd made no attempt to act the part of loving fiancé in front of Jess. He'd looked angry and irritated by her presence and their thanks, and she worried how that would look to Jess.

Especially when she'd made every effort to make it appear they were in love when she'd met his family at their engagement party.

Why had he chosen that precise moment to drop the caring façade he'd hidden behind all week? She'd only just told Jess she loved him and that she was happy to be his wife as well as a mother. Then he'd arrived back at the apartment like an angry lion whose authority had been challenged and made it obvious that the marriage was a deal that was going to unite them and definitely not love.

'I'm not stupid, Em, I know what's going on.' Jess's voice broke through her thoughts.

Emma whirled round to look at her sister and saw a frown of worry creasing her brow. What did she know? That the pregnancy was a mistake and that she'd abandoned her dreams of love and happiness to do what was right for the baby?

'Nothing's going on. Every bride and groom is nervous before the big day.' She bluffed her way out of the corner Jess was backing her into. But it was too late. Emma's fragile faith in her love for Nikolai was fading fast. Was she really doing the right thing by her child, marrying a man who didn't want her around, much less love her?

'Tell me, Em, please.' Her sister's pleas showed wisdom beyond her years, wisdom born out of the hardships they'd faced growing up.

Emma sighed heavily. 'I can't marry him, Jess. I can't marry a man who doesn't want love in his life. But, more than that, I can't live each day waiting for him to reject me and his baby.'

Any further attempt at spilling out her sorry story

was halted as the dress fitters arrived. Emma let them in, amazed at the quantity of dresses that hung wrapped up on the rail they were quickly setting up. The fact that they were here also made what she was doing seem even more real. She was actually going to marry a man who didn't want love in his life, who could never give her what she'd always dreamed of finding.

But he can give Jess a chance to be something.

Emma tried to shrug off those thoughts and walked over to stand by the tall windows. She looked but didn't see the view which usually captivated her so easily as she battled to halt the doubts which were growing by the second. She heard Jess come to stand beside her.

'What makes you say that?' Jess asked, shock obvious in her voice.

'He's never told me how he feels,' Emma said quietly, not quite able to add that he'd already told her he didn't want love, that the deal they'd struck was one which would benefit Jess.

'I don't think it's something men say,' replied Jess confidently, and Emma turned to look at her, finding it odd that she could even smile at such a remark. 'What?'

'Do you actually know what you are saying?' Emma laughed, trying to lighten things up. She shouldn't be talking to Jess like this. Not if she wanted to prevent her ever finding out the exact terms of the deal.

'Of course I do—I watch films, listen to people talk.' Now Jess laughed, but it was edged with relief. Guilt rushed over Emma. She must have worried Jess for a moment.

Emma pushed all her doubts to the back of her mind.

She was doing this for Jess as well as her baby, which meant she couldn't let on how much she doubted her sanity for accepting the terms of the deal.

'What colour do you think?' She strolled over to the rail of bridesmaid dresses and touched a pink one.

'Blue.' Jess joined her. 'You always said blue was your lucky colour.'

'But I thought you liked pink?' Emma was touched by her sister's acknowledgement that it was her day.

'I do, but I want you to have all the luck in the world, so I want blue.'

As Jess spoke, the dress fitters pulled out several dresses, but a pale-blue strapless gown caught hers and Jess's attention at the same time. Moments later, Jess was twirling round the apartment. 'It's a perfect fit. This has to be the one.'

'You look gorgeous, Jess. All grown up.'

'And I am, so you can go off into the sunset with your very own Prince Charming and not worry about me.' The reproach in Jess's voice brought a mixture of tears to Emma's eyes and a soft giggle of happiness.

'I guess I'd better decide on my dress,' said Emma. 'This is so last minute, I can't possibly find one to fit.'

Cream silks blended with white on the rail and Emma didn't know which one to look at first. Should she even have a full-length gown? What about cream? Or should it be white?

'This is the one,' said Jess as she pulled the skirt of a beautiful white gown towards her and grinned. 'Try it on.'

Helped by the fitter, Emma tried on the white lace gown with a strapless bodice that matched Jess's perfectly; it was almost too good to be true. As she was zipped into it, she looked at herself in the mirror and saw, not plain Emma, but a beautiful bride. The dress was simple yet elegant with a small train; she'd never imagined herself in such a dress.

'It's all meant to be,' Jess gushed. 'First my dress, now this one. You and Nikolai are going to make the perfect couple.'

CHAPTER TWELVE

EMMA WOKE EARLY with a start, the big bed cold and empty, just as it had been since the day Jess had arrived and Nikolai had moved into a hotel. He was stepping back from her as if he too had doubts. Why hadn't she tried harder to sort things when they'd been at the hospital?

She looked around her. The early-morning sun shined with wicked brightness into her bedroom, seeming to highlight the wedding dress hanging in readiness for that afternoon, when she would step into it and seal the hardest deal of her life.

Could she do it? Could she put on the white gown of lace and become Nikolai's wife, knowing he would never love her?

She pulled on her jeans and jumper and put on a pair of flat pumps. She couldn't stay and look at the wedding dress any longer. She had to get away, get out of the apartment and think. The sensation that she was doing the wrong thing had taken over, blocking out everything else.

'Where are you going?' Jess asked, quickly taking in her casual clothes as she went into the bedroom.

'I need to go for a walk. I need to think, Jess. I need

to think really hard before I make a terrible mistake.'
Emma looked at the long pale-blue dress she and Jess
had selected the day she'd arrived. It hung in readiness,
mocking, from the wardrobe door. During those few
hours when she'd tried her own dress on for the final
time, Jess had enjoyed herself so much selecting styles
and colours that her enthusiasm had become infectious
and for a while Emma had believed everything was
going to be all right.

But it could never be all right. Nikolai could never
love her as she loved him. If she married him it would
be the worst mistake of her life.

'What's the matter, Em?' Jess crossed the room
quickly and Emma wondered how she was ever going
to tell her. How did you look your sister in the eye and
tell her you were throwing away her chance of fulfill-
ing her dream, of being what she wanted to be, and
worse, subjecting a child to a life without a father?

'I'm not sure I can do this.' Emma felt ill at the concern on her sister's face and wished she hadn't said
anything, but she had to. In about six hours she would
have to put the wedding dress on. What if she couldn't?
What if she couldn't unite herself with Nikolai in marriage? She had to tell Jess something, had to give her
some warning that things weren't as they should be.

'I thought you were happy, that you loved him,' Jess
said, a hint of panic in her voice, and that was the
last thing Emma wanted her sister to do. They'd had
enough panic and upset in their lives. How had this
turned into such a mess?

'I was,' she said with a sigh as she looked past her
sister and to the view of the green trees of the park beyond. 'And I do love him.'

I love him too much and I can't face his rejection.

'So what's wrong, then?' Jess touched her gently on the arm, pulling her back from her thoughts, back to what she had to do.

She closed her eyes against the pain of knowing she'd fallen in love with Nikolai even after he'd readily confessed he couldn't love anyone. She couldn't stop the words any longer, couldn't hold them back. 'He doesn't love me.'

She felt Jess's hand slip from her arm, but she couldn't look at her and tell her what it was all about, why they were really getting married, so pulled away. Even when Jess spoke again she couldn't look at her. She'd failed her. If she ran out on Nikolai now, she'd be throwing away the chance for her baby to know a different life. 'I think you are wrong about that.'

'Don't, Jess, you don't know the half of it.' Emma's hot retort left her lips before she had time to consider what she wanted to say.

'Last night he looked as if he'd wanted to eat you alive.' Jess's bold words, so out of character for her little sister, didn't ease the doubt; instead, it increased it. Lust had been responsible for that look on Nikolai's face. Nothing other than desire-fuelled lust.

'That's not love, Jess, and it's not something to build your future on. Don't ever fall for that.' But wasn't that what she herself had done—fallen for the power of raw lust?

'You're wrong, Em. What I saw in his eyes last night was love. Anyone can see that.'

'Don't be so silly. You're not even seventeen. How can you know what love looks like?' Emma was becoming irritated with this conversation. All she wanted to do was leave the confines of the apartment. She needed time to think what to do next—after she'd told Nikolai they wouldn't be getting married.

'I know it was love, Em, I just know it. He loves you.' Jess pleaded with her, but it was too late. She'd made up her mind. 'Don't let your past stand in the way of your future. You are not Mother and he's not your father.'

That was so painfully close to the truth, she didn't want to hear it. 'I have to get out of here.'

For nearly an hour Emma all but marched around the park but none of it gave her any joy, any release from the feeling of impending doom which loomed over her. All she could think about was that she had to tell Nikolai it was over. She stopped walking and found a bench and, sitting down, took out her phone. Her hands shook and, even though her heart was breaking, it was what she had to do. This sham of an engagement had gone on long enough. It was time to end it.

She pressed Nikolai's number and listened to the ringing tone, part of her wanting him to pick up, part of her wishing he wouldn't, that she could hang up and walk away. The message system took over, and for a moment she nearly ended the call without leaving a message, but if she didn't do this now, didn't say what she needed to, it would be too late. He'd be waiting for her to arrive at the church he'd booked for the small, intimate ceremony with only his family and Jess as guests. They might have struck a cold deal for their child's sake, but she couldn't marry him knowing he'd never love her.

'It's me, Emma,' she said, not liking the quiver in

her voice, and she tried to sound much sterner. The message she left had to be decisive and firm. 'I can't do this, Nikolai. It was wrong of me to accept your deal. I can't marry you. I'm going back to London with Jess—tonight.'

She ended the call and stared at the phone as if it might explode, but inside she knew she'd done the right thing. She couldn't marry a man who didn't love her, not when her love for him grew deeper and stronger each day. All along she'd thought she was doing the right thing, but now she couldn't see any happiness for her or the baby in a loveless marriage.

She looked at the time on her phone: almost ten. The wedding was due to take place at three. Nikolai had plenty of time to sort things out and make all the necessary cancellations, just as she had time to get a flight back to London booked for her and Jess. She hoped he wouldn't come and try and persuade her to go through with the wedding. Would he really do that when marriage and fatherhood were the very things he'd admitted not wanting? She wanted to be able to leave in peace. Of course, they'd have to settle things to do with the baby, but that could wait until she was more in control of her emotions, more able to be strong and hold back her love.

It was what she had to do, but she couldn't move, as if by doing so it would make it worse. But how much worse could it get? She was pregnant with the child of the man she'd lost her heart to and all he wanted was a loveless marriage, a convenient deal. The spark of sexual attraction wouldn't keep the marriage alive for ever, and once it dwindled to nothing she didn't think she could continue to live the lie—or hide her love.

She turned off her phone and as she sat in the peace of the park, letting the birdsong soothe her, she wished she could turn off her emotions as easily. All she needed was a few minutes to compose herself and then she'd go back to the apartment, book the flights and leave New York. She could explain to Jess on the long flight home, admit it had been a mistake to come here, and an even bigger mistake to accept Nikolai's deal, whatever extras he'd thrown her way.

Nikolai tried to get Emma on the phone again as he strode through the park. Jess had told him to try there after he'd called at the apartment. Anger boiled up inside him as he heard her message going round and round in his head. She didn't want to get married. *I can't do this, Nikolai:* that was what she'd said.

Each time he replayed the words in his mind anger sizzled deep inside him. Anger and rejection. He should have seen it coming. What she'd said at the hospital after the scan suddenly made sense. While he'd been bonding with his child and liking the idea of fatherhood, of settling down with Emma, she'd been thinking of ending the engagement and calling off the wedding.

Anger simmered, pushing him to walk hard and fast through the park. He had no idea where to begin looking and savagely pulled out his phone and tried to call her again. Nothing. She'd turned it off. If she thought a switched-off phone would be enough to deter him, she was very much mistaken. He wasn't used to people backing out of a deal and he certainly wasn't accustomed to being denied what he wanted—and he wanted Emma.

The thought trickled through him like a mountain

stream thawing after a long, hard winter. He wanted her, really wanted her. Not just with the hot lust that had driven him mad, but with something much deeper. It wasn't anything to do with the baby. He wanted Emma.

The park was full of morning joggers and dog walkers wrestling with groups of dogs as he stopped and looked around for Emma. She'd been so enamoured with the park since her arrival; she could be anywhere. A strong curse left his lips as he marched on towards the lake; then, as he rounded a corner, he could see her through the trees. She was sitting on a bench, looking away into the distance, totally absorbed in thought.

He reined in the instinct to rush over to her and demand to know just what the message had been all about, and instead walked slowly towards her, taking advantage of the fact that she was looking the other way. Her long hair gleamed in the morning sunshine as he got closer and he rubbed the pads of his thumb and finger together, remembering the silky softness of her hair. Would he ever feel it again?

Emma turned to look his way and he stopped walking, frozen to the spot with something that seemed horribly like fear, but fear of what? He saw the moment she realised it was him, saw the tension make her body stiffen, and the realisation that he did that to her hurt more than he knew. She was either afraid of him or hated him for what he'd done to her.

She didn't move, but she did look down, as she always did when something was difficult to do. Was her reluctance to leave an invitation for him to join her? He didn't care what the hell it was. He was going to sit with her regardless.

I can't let the woman I love walk out on me.

That thought crashed into him and he stopped again, his heart pounding as he realised exactly what that thought meant. He'd felt the same at the hospital. Why hadn't he seen it then?

He looked at her, sitting on the bench in the morning sunshine only a short distance away, yet it was like a chasm had opened up right there in the park. It yawned between them, becoming greater with each passing second.

He couldn't move, couldn't cross it.

He'd pushed her to the other side of it right from the very beginning and she'd been more than happy to be there. She'd agreed with everything he'd said about commitment and love, accepted the cold terms of his marriage deal. She scorned love or happy-ever-after just as much as he had, but now, as if he'd finally opened his eyes and seen what was real, he had to accept that he did want all that. He did want Emma in his life, as his wife and the mother of his baby, but not out of any obligation—out of love.

Did he risk everything and tell her how he felt, that he loved her after all he'd said to her? Or did he try and persuade her to keep the deal in the hope he'd got it wrong? Maybe panic had filled his head with such nonsense as love.

But he didn't just feel that desolate distance in his head. He felt it in his chest—in his heart. That sensation he'd experienced since the moment he'd first met Emma was back, squeezing tighter than ever, as if trying to get him to acknowledge the truth, acknowledge it as love.

She looked at him, apprehension clear on her face, and finally he managed to move towards her. Each step was harder than the previous one. How could he tell her what he really felt when he'd only just realised the truth of it himself?

'Did you think a quick phone message would be enough to extricate you from our deal?' That wasn't what he wanted to say at all, but the protective barrier around his heart wasn't just keeping her out, it was locking the truth inside him, preventing him from saying what he had to say, what he wanted to say.

She looked up at him as he came to stand in front of her, those gorgeous green eyes narrowing against the sun. Or was it the harshness in his voice? 'I didn't expect you not to answer.'

'I was in the shower,' he said quickly, banishing the memories of the time they had spent in the shower together not so many days ago.

She looked down and away from him again. Was she recalling the same thing, the same heated passion? He sat down next to her and once again her gaze met his. 'It doesn't matter, Nikolai, because I can't marry you.'

'Not even for the baby?' He flung the question at her as he clenched his teeth against the panic which flowed through him like a river in flood. He couldn't let her go, let her just walk out of his life, not now he knew what he really felt for her. How long had he loved her? The thought barely materialised before he knew the answer. He'd loved her from the first night they'd spent together in Vladimir, maybe even the first moment he'd seen her.

'No.' She shook her head and looked directly ahead of her, as if distracted by the surroundings, but he sensed she was holding back on him. But why? And what?

* * *

Emma looked at the pain in his eyes and knew he was blaming his past, his father's mistakes. Her heart wrenched and she desperately wanted to reach out to him, to reassure him it was nothing to do with that. But, if she did, she'd weaken and the last thing she wanted to blurt out was that she couldn't marry anyone who didn't love her as she loved them, that she couldn't put herself in the path of such rejection.

'No. I know it sounds very clichéd, but it's me.' She looked into his eyes, seeing their darkness harder than they'd ever been.

'So you are quite happy to back out of our deal.' His voice was deceptively calm and that unsettled her even more. Was he just going through the motions of asking her to reconsider when he'd rather book flights back to London for Jess and her himself?

'For our child's sake, yes.' She skirted around the truth, her heart pounding harder than ever, and despite the warm spring sun she shivered as skitters of apprehension slithered down her spine.

'Our child will benefit from the marriage, but will it benefit from being brought up by you alone, while I am on the other side of the world?' The scorn in that question was almost too much for her. Was he deliberately trying to make it harder for her or was he finding a way to make her worst nightmare come true and take her baby from her?

Whatever he was doing, this had to be sorted now. She couldn't go on for the rest of her pregnancy wondering what he would do next. 'Our baby will be better off with two parents who are apart and happy than two living under the same roof that are unhappy.'

'And will you be happy?' The question threw her off guard, as did the change of his tone. He sounded defeated. She'd never heard Nikolai sound like that.

'All I want is for my child to grow up happy, to never feel the sting of rejection from its father.' She wanted to say more, to make him aware just how anxious she was, but stopped the words and the pain from flowing out.

'And you think I will reject my son or daughter?' Hurt resounded in his voice, but his eyes narrowed with annoyance. 'After all I saw and witnessed as a child, do you really think I want to hurt my own child?'

She looked down, knowing her words had been taken the wrong way, and she hated herself for hurting him. He'd done all a young boy could to protect his mother and even now, as a grown man, was doing the same. That was why he'd insisted on the pretence of love at the engagement party and why he'd gone to Vladimir in the first instance.

Instinctively she reached out to him, placing her hand on his arm. 'No, Nikolai, that's not what I thought. I don't want my child to know what I've known. I can't stand by and let you reject them when they are no longer any use in your life.'

He took her hand in his, the warmth of it briefly chasing the apprehension away 'I would never do that, Emma, never.'

She looked at him as his eyes softened and she almost lost her resolve, but his next words brought it hurtling back to her.

'I'm not about to let you walk away. I want to see my child grow up and, just as I never want to be like my father, I promise I will never do what yours has done to you.'

'It doesn't mean we should marry, though.'

'We will marry as planned, Emma.' He looked at his watch. 'In less than four hours, you will be my wife.'

CHAPTER THIRTEEN

'I'M SORRY, NIKOLAI.' Emma jumped up away from him, breaking the tenuous connection he'd just forged. Her hard words hit him like a speeding truck. 'It's too late.'

He watched as she stood up and looked down at him and, when he couldn't respond, couldn't say what he wanted her to hear, she turned and began to walk away. It seemed as if he was watching each step she took happen in slow motion, but each one took her further from him.

He couldn't let that happen. She couldn't walk away from him until he'd told her what he'd only just realised himself. Nerves sparked through him, briefly making it impossible to say or do anything except watch her begin to walk away.

'Emma, wait.' The demand in his voice rang clearly through the morning air but she didn't slow, didn't turn. She was leaving him, walking out of his life. He had to make her see reason, had to make her understand, and there was only one way to do that.

He walked briskly after her, catching up with her as she began to cross Bow Bridge. 'I need you, Emma.'

Had he said that aloud? He stood still at the end of the bridge and watched as her steps faltered, then she stood, her back to him in the middle of the bridge. Seconds ticked by but it felt like hours as he waited for her to turn to look at him. When she did, he could see she was upset, see she was on the verge of tears, and he hated himself for it. He'd handled this all wrong, right from the moment he'd woken after that first night they'd spent together. The night that had changed not only their lives but him.

'Don't say what you don't mean, Nikolai.'

'I mean it, Emma, I need you.' Inside his head a voice was warning him that that wasn't enough, that he had to say more, he had to put himself on the line and tell her he loved her. He couldn't do that, not knowing she loved another man, but it was his baby she was carrying and he'd been the only man who'd made love to her. Surely that meant something?

'It's not enough,' she said firmly, her chin lifting in defiance. 'I want more than that, Nikolai. I want to be needed for who I am, not for the baby I carry. But more than that I need love.'

His stomach plummeted as she said those final words. Was she going back to London to be with Richard? Did she love him that much?

'I always thought love was nothing more than a word.' He took a step towards her. That chasm he'd felt earlier now had the thinnest of wires across it, but could he use it? Did he have the courage to reveal his emotions when they were still shockingly new to him?

'You made that more than clear from the very beginning.' Still she stood there in the middle of the bridge, looking at him with fierce determination. She didn't even notice a couple walking across the bridge towards him. Her gaze didn't leave his face for one second.

He had done exactly that; there was no denying he'd made it absolutely clear he didn't want love. Such a denial was what had kept him safe. It meant he'd never have to give a piece of himself to someone who could use it and destroy him emotionally—something Emma had had the power to do from the moment they'd first met. As a teenager he'd spoken just once about his father to his mother and she had confessed she'd loved him when they'd first met, before he'd shown his true self. From that moment on he'd vowed to keep such destructive emotions as love locked away.

He couldn't do that any longer. He had to acknowledge them and set them free, even if Emma did have the power to destroy him. If she didn't feel the same burning love for him, then he would be nothing, but he couldn't just tell her, not when he wanted her to be happy—with or without him. If she truly loved someone else, then he would have to let her go. It shook him to the core to realise he loved her enough to do that, enough to set her free into the arms of another man.

He thought back to their discussion on love, to the day she'd laughed at such a notion existing. It had been that denial of what she'd truly wanted that had forged the path forward for them.

'You made a joke out of love and happiness. You scorned it as much as I did, Emma.' He took several tentative steps closer, encouraged when she didn't move, didn't turn and walk away. Inside, his heart was breaking. He was a mess, but he kept his stern control, retaining that ever-present defensive shield.

'I can understand why you want to shut love out of your life, Nikolai, but the things I experienced as a child made me want that kind of happiness even more.'

She took a step towards him and hope soared inside him. 'We want different things. You want to be free of commitment and emotion, but I want love, Nikolai.'

Those last words goaded him harder than he could have imagined, pushing him to ask just what he needed to know, even though the answer would be like a knife in his newly revealed heart. 'And does Richard give you that love?'

'Richard?' Emma's mind whirled in shock. Why did Richard have anything to do with this? She struggled to think, struggled to work out how he'd come to that conclusion, and then it hit her as she remembered their afternoon on the river trip. She'd taken a call from Richard and had been so happy the article was out and that he liked it, approved of what she'd done, but Nikolai's mood had darkened the instant she'd told him who was on the phone. She'd thought he was angry with her, but was it something more? Had he felt threatened by Richard, even though he'd been on the phone?

That wretched flicker of hope flared to life within her once more and kept her where she was. She looked at Nikolai, standing now at the end of Bow Bridge, as if to continue to walk towards her was something he couldn't do.

'Do you love him, Emma? Is he the man you are leaving to go back to?' Nikolai's voice was hoarse with heavy emotion in a way she'd never heard before.

She blinked at him in total shock. He seriously thought she was in love with Richard? *You used to, before he rejected that young love and adoration.* The taunt echoed in her head and she saw it from Nikolai's perspective. She saw the easy friendship she and Richard had established over the last few years, saw how it might look to someone on the outside. But, like Nikolai, Richard had made it more than clear he didn't want anything serious, squashing that first crush until it withered and died, leaving nothing but friendship—a working friendship.

'Richard and I are just friends. Always have been.' She frowned at the scowl which crossed his face. Did such a reaction really mean he saw Richard as a threat? But to what—their marriage born out of a deal or something more?

'But that isn't what you want, is it, Emma? You told me as much on the boat.'

'I did?'

'"It hurts like hell to feel anything for someone who feels nothing for you". Those were your exact words, Emma.' He calmly repeated what she'd told him, his dark eyes watching every move she made, every breath she took.

Emma's knees almost buckled beneath her and she moved to the side of the bridge, clutching at the ornate balustrades for support. She'd been talking about him, not Richard, but he'd interpreted it as something quite different. No wonder he'd become distant to the point of coldness since that day. The closeness they'd begun to share, which she'd hoped would give rise to love, had vanished—because of what she'd said.

Waves of nausea rushed over her and her head swam. She couldn't think any more, could barely stand. She hadn't eaten anything yet, too anxious earlier to face anything, and now it was all too much. She couldn't do this now.

She felt as though she was falling then strong arms folded around her as Nikolai wrapped her in the safety of his embrace. To feel his arms around her, holding her against his body, was almost unbearable. It was like coming home—and it broke her heart a little bit more.

'You're not well.' The deep, seductive timbre of his voice radiated through her and she closed her eyes, allowing herself a brief moment in the haven of his embrace.

'Maybe we can talk later.' She clutched at the lifeline the moment had given her, not wanting to have this discussion any more. It was bad enough that he didn't love her, that he was about to reject her, but to accuse her of loving Richard was too much.

'No, we talk now—or not at all.' She looked up into his dark eyes and saw myriad emotions swirling in them, emotions she'd never seen in them before. 'It's your choice, Emma.'

She didn't want to talk now, didn't feel well enough to think, let alone talk, but she couldn't walk away and say nothing. Not when he held her so gently and looked at her so longingly. Was it possible he did feel something for her? Could it ever be love?

She needed to make herself clear, to let him know how wrong he'd got it all. She looked up at his handsome face, fighting the urge to reach up and touch his cheek, feel the smoothness of his freshly shaven face. 'It wasn't Richard I was talking about that day.'

Nikolai had moved quickly, taking Emma in his arms, holding her against him before she'd slithered completely to the floor. He'd inhaled her sweet scent, felt the warmth of her body, and his senses had exploded despite the worry he had for her health. How had he not seen it before? How could he not have known he loved her?

Because you shut your heart away.

She leant against the balustrade and looked up at him, as if waiting for him to say something, expectation mingling with desperation in her eyes. She'd just spoken, as his mind had whirled and his body had gone into overdrive just from holding her. Whatever it was she'd said, she obviously expected a response, but his ability to think rationally had left him the moment he'd held her.

'What did you just say?' he asked gently, unable to resist the urge to brush her hair from her face and then stroke the silky length of it down her back.

She looked up at him, tears beginning to brim in her eyes. 'I said that it wasn't Richard. When I said that on the boat, it wasn't him I was talking about.'

His hand stilled at her back and he held his breath, willing her to say more, but she looked down, her head dipping against his chest. If it wasn't Richard, who was it that didn't love her in the way she loved him? Had she been referring to him? Was it possible she loved him?

'Emma,' he said and lifted her chin forcing her look up at him. 'Have you ever told that person you love them?'

Still he couldn't say that he loved her, couldn't admit his deepest emotion. She searched his face, her gaze flicking over every part of him, as if committing him to her memory in the same way a camera did at the touch of a button.

She shook her head. 'It's not what he wants to hear. He doesn't believe love exists—at least, not for him. I could never tell him. I just can't.'

There was nothing else to do. He had to prove he loved her by telling her right now just how much. He had to risk having got it wrong, risk making a fool of himself. If he didn't tell her he loved her now, he'd lose her for ever.

'Maybe he just has to tell you,' he said as he looked deep into her eyes, the tears now dissolved and hope glowing from them. 'Maybe he needs to be bold and admit something he'd never thought possible.'

'Maybe he does,' she said as she watched his lips, as if willing him to say it, and his heart began to thump hard with trepidation.

He took a deep breath and swallowed, trying to instil calm into his body. This was the one thing he thought he'd never say. 'I love you, Emma Sanders. Completely and utterly.'

She closed her eyes, her body relaxed in his embrace and he couldn't resist her any longer. The temptation to kiss her was too much and he lowered his head and pressed his lips against hers. The soft sigh which escaped her did untold things to his body, but passion and desire could wait. This was a kiss of love.

Emma sighed as Nikolai kissed her, so tenderly it almost made her cry. He loved her. It wasn't only that he'd told her, but it was the way he was kissing her which proved it more than anything else. This kiss was different. It wasn't hot and filled with lustful desire that stoked the fire of passion within her. This kiss was very different. It was gentle and, more importantly, it was loving.

She wrapped her arms around his neck and kissed him back, finally allowing all the love she felt to pour from her. He stopped kissing her and pressed his forehead to hers, the gesture so unguarded emotionally she couldn't say what she wanted to say for a moment.

'I thought you didn't want love.' She smiled, her voice teasing and light.

'That was before I met you. Everything changed the moment you stepped off that train in Vladimir.' His eyes were so tender, so filled with love, it was heart-rending and his voice broke with intense huskiness that sent a wave of pleasure breaking over her.

She closed her eyes and revisited the memory of the day they'd met, but even more importantly the knowledge that he had felt something for her from the moment they had met seeped into her. It had been no different for her. There had been something between them from that very first moment at the station in Vladimir, and he'd admitted that had turned to love even before she'd been carrying his child. That could mean only one thing.

'So our child was conceived out of love, Nikolai.' She breathed the words against his lips as he once more claimed them in a deep and meaningful kiss, his hands holding her face as if he couldn't bear not to kiss her.

Around her life went on: voices of people in the park, the ripple of the water beneath them and birds singing their joy of spring all blended into the most perfect backdrop for the moment the man she loved with all her heart confessed his love for her.

As he pulled back from her, she let her palms slide down to his chest, feeling the beat of his heart beneath her right palm, a heart which was filled with love for her. He'd had the courage to admit his love even though he'd been convinced she was going to walk away from him. How had she got it all so wrong?

'I love you, Nikolai Cunningham—with all my heart.' She smiled up at him as he smiled back at her, then kissed her tenderly, his lips gentle and loving. She wanted to melt into the moment, enjoy the kiss, but she needed him to know how much his words meant to her. She pushed against his body and pulled away from him, away from the temptation to deepen the kiss.

'You have no idea how relieved I am to hear that. The thought that you were in love with another man has been eating me up for days.' His deep, sexy voice held a hint of seriousness and she knew it had been hard for him to talk about his feelings, no matter what they were.

'Is that why you really moved out of the apartment?' she asked as shyness crept over her. 'I thought you wanted me out of your life.'

'Like your father? No, Emma, that will never happen. I figured I needed all the luck I could get after what Jess had said, so didn't want to tempt fate by flouting tradition. I knew even then I couldn't risk losing you, but I was too blinded by my past to realise why—that I'd fallen in love with you.'

'Really?' She looked up at him to see amusement sparkling in his eyes, mixing with the newly acknowledged love.

'Yes, but I also wanted you and Jess to have time to catch up and have girl chats about me.' The laughter in his voice was contagious; she laughed softly and when he stroked her hair back from her face she almost melted all over again.

Then what he'd said finally registered and embarrassment flooded her. 'You heard us talking?'

How much had he heard? She recalled telling Jess she loved him with all her heart, and she'd meant it, but they wouldn't be here like this, with the worry of the last few days behind them, if he had truly heard what she and Jess had spoken about.

'Only a little bit,' he said and his brows rose, his eyes filling with that sexy amusement that had captured her heart in the first place.

'Well, you obviously didn't hear the part where I told Jess I loved you so much that it almost hurt; that marrying you was what I wanted to do,' she said with an impish smile on her lips, taunting him mercilessly.

The humour left his face. 'No, I didn't hear that, but it could have saved me a lot of heartache if I had.'

She laughed softly, wanting to lighten the mood. 'I'd much rather just tell you myself.'

'In that case, don't let me stop you.' He pulled her against him once more and pressed his lips briefly to hers.

'I love you, Nikolai, so very much, I just want to marry you. Today.'

'Is that so?' he teased. 'In that case, you are in luck; I have everything planned for a perfect wedding for the woman I love.'

She looked at her watch and let out a shocked gasp. 'I have to go now. The man I love with all my heart is going to make me his wife and the happiest woman alive. I just hope he'll be there waiting for me.'

'I have every faith that he will be, because he's madly in love with you.'

EPILOGUE

EMMA PULLED ON an elegant black gown and looked at her reflection. The last time she'd studied herself so intensely had been the day she'd tried on her wedding dress. Now, over a year later, she was a mother to a beautiful little boy and so happy the doubts she'd had in the days before her wedding seemed like a bad dream.

'As ever, you look amazing, Mrs Cunningham.' Nikolai kissed the back of her neck and looked into the mirror at her. The usual flood of love for him filled her and she smiled back at him as he continued to compliment her. 'It will be an honour to escort you to the ballet tonight.'

A quiver of apprehension ran through her as she thought of Jess being given a chance to dance as the lead ballerina so early in her career. 'I hope Jess isn't too nervous. This is her first leading role.'

'And what better place than here in Russia, at its greatest school? She is the rising star of the company. She will have a wonderful life.' Nikolai's reassurance helped to quell the nerves she had for Jess and she knew he was right.

Emma still couldn't believe that Jess was now half-way through her training and already other ballet companies were interested in offering her a place. She had the world at her feet. It was more than she could ever have hoped for her baby sister.

'I do wish we could have brought Nathan.' Emma turned to Nikolai, wrapping herself into his embrace.

'He is just fine with his grandma.' Nikolai kissed her gently—stirring sensations she couldn't allow to take over moments before they were due to leave the hotel. She blamed it on how amazingly sexy Nikolai was in a tuxedo.

'But it's the first time we've left New York without him.' She smiled as his brows rose in a suggestive way, hinting at the plans he had to fill that time without a six-month-old baby making demands on their attention.

'Which is precisely why I intend to take full advantage of the fact. Once we've seen Jess in her starring role, I intend to bring you back to this room and that very large bed. I want to make love to you all night, just to make sure you know exactly how much and how completely I love you.'

'Is that wise?' Emma teased as she kissed his freshly shaven cheek, not daring to press her lips to his.

'What makes you ask that?' His eyes darkened with desire and an answering heat scorched inside her.

She shrugged nonchalantly. 'You know what happened last time we made love in Russia…'

'This time will be different,' he said as he kissed the back of her neck. She watched him in the mirror until she had to close her eyes against the pleasure.

'In what way?' she asked in a teasing voice.

'This time you will know how much I love you with each and every kiss.'

She turned in his arms and looked up into his handsome face, hardly able to believe how happy she was. 'Everything you do for me, Nikolai, shows me that— from bringing me here to see Jess dance, to supporting me with my photography. I couldn't be happier.'

'But I'd still like to show you,' he said softly.

'Then who am I to argue?' She laughed up at him.

Nikolai looked down at her, a seriousness brushing away the humour of moments ago. 'You are my wife, the mother of my son and the woman I love with all my heart.'

* * * * *

If you enjoyed this story, check out these other great reads from Rachael Thomas
MARRIED FOR THE ITALIAN'S HEIR
TO BLACKMAIL A DI SIONE
THE SHEIKH'S LAST MISTRESS

And don't miss these other
ONE NIGHT WITH CONSEQUENCES
themed stories

THE GUARDIAN'S VIRGIN WARD
by Caitlin Crews

CLAIMING HIS CHRISTMAS CONSEQUENCE
by Michelle Smart

Available now!

MILLS & BOON®

MODERN™

POWER, PASSION AND IRRESISTIBLE TEMPTATION

MILLS & BOON®

EXCLUSIVE EXTRACT

Even unsentimental Alessandro Di Sione can't deny
his grandfather's dream of retrieving a scandalous
painting. Yet its return depends on outspoken Princess
Gabriella. Travelling together to locate the painting,
Gabby is drawn to this guilt-ridden man.
Could their passion be his salvation?

Read on for a sneak preview of
THE LAST DI SIONE CLAIMS HIS PRIZE

Alessandro was so different than she was. Gabby had
never truly fully appreciated just how different men and
women were. In a million ways, big and small.

Yes, there was the obvious, but it was more than that.
And it was those differences that suddenly caused her to
glory in who she was, what she was. To feel, if only for
a moment, that she completely understood herself both
body and soul, and that they were united in one desire.

"Kiss me, Princess," he said, his voice low, strained.

He was affected.

So she had won.

She had been the one to make him burn.

But she'd made a mistake if she'd thought this game
had one winner and one loser. She was right down there
with him. And she didn't care about winning anymore.

She couldn't deny him, not now. Not when he was
looking at her like she was a woman and not a girl, or
an owl. Not when he was looking at her like she was

the sun, moon and all the stars combined. Bright, brilliant and something that held the power to hold him transfixed.

Something more than what she was. Because Gabriella D'Oro had never transfixed anyone. Not her parents. Not a man.

But he was looking at her like she mattered. She didn't feel like shrinking into a wall, or melting into the scenery. She wanted him to keep looking.

She didn't want to hide from this. She wanted all of it.

Slowly, so slowly, so that she could savor the feel of him, relish the sensations of his body beneath her touch, she slid her hand up his throat, feeling the heat of his skin, the faint scratch of whiskers.

Then she moved to cup his jaw, his cheek.

"I've never touched a man like this before," she confessed.

And she wasn't even embarrassed by the confession, because he was still looking at her like he wanted her.

He moved closer, covering her hand with his. She could feel his heart pounding heavily, could sense the tension running through his frame. "I've touched a great many women," he said, his tone grave. "But at the moment it doesn't seem to matter."

That was when she kissed him.

MP0117_2

MILLS & BOON®

Why shop at millsandboon.co.uk?

Each year, thousands of romance readers find their perfect read at millsandboon.co.uk. That's because we're passionate about bringing you the very best romantic fiction. Here are some of the advantages of shopping at www.millsandboon.co.uk:

* **Get new books first**—you'll be able to buy your favourite books one month before they hit the shops

* **Get exclusive discounts**—you'll also be able to buy our specially created monthly collections, with up to 50% off the RRP

* **Find your favourite authors**—latest news, interviews and new releases for all your favourite authors and series on our website, plus ideas for what to try next

* **Join in**—once you've bought your favourite books, don't forget to register with us to rate, review and join in the discussions

Visit **www.millsandboon.co.uk**
for all this and more today!